Battling Spirits & Kindly Hearts

Steven Baker

The Book Guild Ltd

First published in Great Britain in 2016 by
The Book Guild Ltd
9 Priory Business Park
Wistow Road, Kibworth
Leicestershire, LE8 0RX
Freephone: 0800 999 2982
www.bookguild.co.uk
Email: info@bookguild.co.uk
Twitter: @bookguild

Typeset in Aldine401 BT

Printed and bound in Great Britain by CPI Group (UK) Ltd, Croydon, CR0 4YY

ISBN 978 1910878 910

British Library Cataloguing in Publication Data.
A catalogue record for this book is available from the British Library.

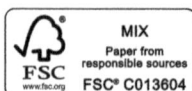

For the nurses and doctors of Worthing Hospital and the University College Hospital, London, who helped me survive cancer in 2013

Prologue

In 1939 Michael Forbes is twelve-years-old and living with his struggling parents, Frank and Honeysuckle in Grenadier Guard Road in the heart of London's East End. Frank is a man in ill-health who toils away in a sauce factory trying to earn enough for the upkeep of his beloved family. Honeysuckle is the heart and soul of the family providing love and support for Frank and Michael. They are so accustomed to hardship that they believe this to be their natural way of life. The one bright light on the horizon is the hop picking season in Kent which they all look forward to immensely. Frank is frustrated and unhappy with his lot in life and yearns for something better for his family. Sadly the advent of war and the London Blitz puts paid to any ambitions he has of bettering his life.

With the onset of war along with many children of the time Michael is evacuated to Australia where he will live for nearly six years. His Aunt Doris has married an Australian farmer called Jack Hope and moved to Endeavour Downs Station in the outback of New South Wales. It is there that Michael spends the war years. His life is reshaped completely as he meets colourful and larger than life personalities. He endures experiences maturing him beyond his years. The story culminates in a spectacular drive from New South Wales to Queensland.

Years later back home in England, Michael Forbes remembers the days of his East End childhood, the hop picking season of 1939, and the years spent on a cattle station in Australia. In particular he remembers the people of his youth who were so influential. They are the battling spirits and kindly hearts of this story.

One

Somewhere beyond the swirling mists of time there is a land that once visited can never be returned to. It is a place that is distant in terms of years and generations rather than miles. Like a mysterious uncharted island on a sparkling ocean obscured by volcanic ash and the mist from tropical rain clouds it is a place vastly different to anywhere else in the world we may travel to. It is the land of childhood. The past is indeed a different country.

Maybe it was a beautiful place for some, a time of great happiness and nostalgia filled with family laughter and friendship. Perhaps for others it was a time of sorrow; the starkness of haunted faces and poverty, raised angry voices and floods of tears. It may even have been a combination of all these things. Life is a series of events controlled by the fates and circumstances that often intervene and disrupt the carefully made plans each and every one of us has.

Let us go back in time to the great city of London in 1939. It was not the multi-cultural neon-lit metropolis that it is today with all manner and races of people making their way through a city containing the historical architecture of Sir Christopher Wren and upwardly soaring art deco buildings intermingling ancient and nouveau-riche.

This was a London that had only recently begun to recover from the harsh years of the Great Depression. Class and privilege was very evident while working people referred to as lower class often lived in poverty-stricken circumstances. Millions of people had suffered through unemployment. In 1936 the Jarrow March of the unemployed to London took place. The tide was turning in so many respects.

The rise of fascism in Europe had created tension and unrest bringing with it a sense of grim expectancy that war was imminent. Civil war in Spain had served as a dress rehearsal for World War Two that would last six long years. The warnings that Winston Churchill and Anthony Eden had given about the threat to peace posed by Hitler's rise were sadly to come true.

All of this seemed a long way from a soot-grey, dark terraced street called Grenadier Guard Road. This was where twelve-year-old Michael Forbes lived with his parents Frank and Honeysuckle. Back in his childhood days no-one in the street ever seemed to lock their front door. Almost as a matter of tradition women scrubbed the front doorstep and polished the brass handle doorknockers each day. All of their neighbours and friends were working people who lived close to the breadline. Few people he knew ever wore good suits or had money to spare but smiles and laughter were plentiful. There were tears although the occasions that spawned them were rare. Generosity of spirit was in abundance. If a neighbour had a problem it became something shared. When there was a little bit of luck or a reason to celebrate it was guaranteed that someone in the street would hold a party to which everyone came.

Like many men in later years Michael would reflect on those childhood times. The curious thing was that he would remember nothing but the good about it. Somehow the sad things and frustrations paled into insignificance and blended into an aching nostalgia for that distant era. It was a time of warm family togetherness that was to be shattered by the long years of war.

There was a glorious summer that year. Portsmouth won the FA Cup. The charismatic Irishman Jack Doyle fought against the robust Eddie Philips in a crowd-pulling boxing match at the White City Stadium. Life went on as normally as possible in the nervous circumstances of a looming war.

Michael Forbes envisaged that he would spend all the days of his life in London. Until then he thought, as his father did, that it was the most magical place to have been raised. A city that could boast Trafalgar Square, Piccadilly Circus, the Albert & Victoria Museum, the Houses of Parliament at Westminster, Buckingham Palace and The Mall with a daily Changing of the Guard must surely have been unsurpassable anywhere in the world.

The London that Michael knew as a boy was not the one of Mayfair, Sloane Square, or the glittering area that was always spoken of as being 'up West'. No, that part of the world where the champagne corks popped and the toffs danced to the music of Ambrose and Harry Roy was a very long way from the life he knew. A South African-born singer called Al Bowlly thrilled the masses when he sang the song about the Great Depression,

'Buddy can you spare a dime'. But the plush nightclubs where Al sang and the areas of life that his song depicted were light years apart.

Michael's boyhood home in Grenadier Guard Road was situated in the real pulsating heart of London's East End. His parents were both born within the sound of Bow Bells. A generation later he was also blessed with the same privilege when he was born. The world that he knew as a lad was the area between the markets in Petticoat Lane and the docks where ships sailed out to all corners of the world. The neighbourhood he lived in was a place where the people worked in the markets, on the dockside, and in some of the industrial sprawls. Most of the local populous were ordinary struggling Londoners. Some came from a variety of different ethnic backgrounds. There were Polish, Jewish, Italian and Irish families as well as descendants from the Huguenots. All of them added colour and character to the area.

When he was a boy, Petticoat Lane markets held a magnetic fascination. There was an indefinable magic about the mass of people congregating in the narrow spaces between the different stalls; the sounds of the warm friendly cries of the Cockney salesmen and barrow boys; the shouting and bartering of fishmongers; the meat salesmen, hot pie and jellied eel stands, and the cheery voices of sweet stall ladies. Not only was it the sound of the voices of another age that stayed in the memory but also the mixed aromas of various food stalls intermingled with straw and newspaper, fruit and vegetables, packing cases, pet shops and puppy dogs.

The Forbes' family home in Grenadier Guard Road was one of a long line of boxed-in terrace houses and grey damp council buildings with large families often occupying two or three rooms. Nearly all the dwellings in those narrow streets were in a run-down condition, more fit for destruction than inhabitation. Close by there were factories and a railway line with a huge train carriage workshop and a goods siding.

At the end of the street was the British Grenadier public house. In the Thirties it had quite a reputation. This was a venue where the local major and minor criminal element would gather under the watchful eye of its landlord, Stan Mills, himself a former wrestler. In those days its clientele included: wide boys, smart suits, racing tipsters, cardsharps and suave pencil-moustached spivs with good looking women hanging on to every word like a privileged and adoring audience.

Local infamous villains with names like Joe Lucky, Fuzzy Davies,

Louis Malone and Alf Maguire held court in the snug. They were hard men in good suits who doffed their trilby hats to passers-by and were kind to old ladies but carried razors in their pockets ready for any unexpected altercation. Each man had a history of crime that was well known to the police. They also had a territory each considered their own patch.

Joe Lucky was Russian by birth. His real name was Josephe Luchenya. When Cossacks had destroyed the village of his childhood his parents took the family to England in 1906. He was eight-years-old. A group of Russian emigrants lived near Sidney Street and the Luchenya family set up home close by. In 1912 a siege between anarchists and the police took place in Sidney Street. Crowds gathered to watch. Among them were Joseph and his father. Soon the Scots Guards were called in to bolster support while Winston Churchill, then a young government minister, paid a surprise visit to the scene. Joe Lucky descended into a life of crime and in time became the leader of a gang who worked the racecourses and carried out illegal betting scams.

Fuzzy Davies had a team of crooks who believed they had a monopoly on the docks. Whatever they could get hold of from berthing ships in the way of liquor, spirits, meat, sugar, fruit, clothing, cigarettes, contraband and drugs soon found its way into the hands of local suppliers.

Louis Malone was not yet thirty but active in crime since he was fourteen. He posed as a respectable businessman. The police knew otherwise. Malone ran several boxing clubs, gambling dens, sly grog shops and rumour had it received a regular supply of protection money to finance his enterprises. Cunning and sly he was also dangerous and charming: A deadly mixture. The area he controlled was nicknamed 'The Alley'. On one occasion he and a very tough opponent fought a marathon fist fight. It lasted almost an hour and took place across several streets, through two pubs and a café, inside a dance hall and in a casino, eventually ending up in a back alley. Technically it was a draw but both men were a match for the other. Each was b bloodied and battered.

Alf Maguire was a scrap metal merchant but led a secret life as a bank robber and safe breaker. He was a bagman for all three gang leaders and would later die in prison. Alf was married to a formidable lady called May, the mother of his five children. When he died May Maguire became something of a matriarch amongst the local villains. Their world was a dark sinister one of late nights and shadows, muffled voices, fast cars and shady characters who had a presence that spelt fear. The hard cold existence they survived in was a long way from the other locals.

Just about all of the children Michael went to school with had parents who worked in one of the nearby factories. The biggest was the raincoat factory which manufactured beautiful macs few families in that area could ever afford to buy. There was a tyre factory where the workers used to come home with the stench of rubber clinging to their clothes. Along the road there was a shirt factory, a biscuit factory, and then there was one huge monstrosity of a building. This was a hot steamy food factory where Frank Forbes worked six days a week, shift after shift until he was worn out and at the end of his labours, gratefully escaped to his home in Grenadier Guard Road.

Frank Forbes was in his middle forties then but years of intolerable working conditions, long hours, incessant smoking and poor health had aged him considerably. His face had a sad, tired, dispirited appearance ingrained in his features and his eyes were red with a glimmer of hurt in them. But the pained demeanour concealed a man with a loving heart, a good sense of humour and a quick and ready smile. Life had always been hard graft for him. It seemed he had spent years counting pennies, being either out of work or toiling away for long unsociable hours. Yet he never let things weigh down on him too much. He laughed at Max Miller, the Crazy Gang or Wilson, Keppel and Betty. At any social gathering he could be the life and soul of any party. There was an element of pathos about Frank. In the flash of an instant his face could change from one containing sadness to that of the mirth of a clown.

Most mornings in the house began with Frank going off to work as the sun began to rise, if indeed there was any sun rising on those cold frosty days. Michael always waved to his father from the bedroom window. He would rub away at the frost on the icy cold pane. Down below Frank would wave to him and smile cheerily. Sometimes Michael would hear his father cough as he left the house. It was a terrible deep bronchial cough. His persistent smoking probably aggravated it.

One morning shortly before his thirteenth birthday Michael rose to have breakfast. With the news in Europe looking increasingly grim all the family expected their lives to change along with everybody else. However that morning his mother looked particularly happy. She was singing to herself and winked at him as he came into the kitchen. Honeysuckle smiled effervescently at Michael as she put a bowl of porridge in front of him. At forty-one she was a cheerful and jovial woman with a friendly happy face; she was 5 ft 4 inches with fair hair turning to grey and was also the rock that kept the Forbes family together.

'You will never guess what young Michael!' Honeysuckle exclaimed, pausing to take a sip of tea as she sat down at the table. He looked at her in anticipation. 'Your Auntie Doris is getting married!'

Doris was Frank's younger sister who had just passed her thirtieth birthday. She was an absolutely lovely lady in Michael's eyes who the family always looked forward to seeing. Doris had moved to Kent during the Depression to find work. There she had found employment on a farm milking cows and picking vegetables.

'Getting married?' Michael looked at his mother in surprise. Subconsciously because Doris had held out for so long the family had come to believe she would never marry. 'Who is she going to marry then, Mum?'

'A man from Australia called Jack Hope. He's a smashing bloke I believe. She met him at a barn dance in that village in Kent she lives in.' Honeysuckle poured them both another cup of tea. 'He came over here a few years ago to learn about English farms. His grandfather came from Eltham. He's got a place of his own out there, somewhere in the bush, a farm and an orchard.'

'Where are they going to live Mum?' Michael asked. For one curious moment he half imagined they would move into their already crowded rooms.

Honeysuckle's face took on a trace of downcast expression momentarily. 'Out there. In Australia.' Then just as quickly she smiled and ruffled Michael's hair. 'I will miss her. Mind you, all that sun and blue skies. The chance to start a new life. Wouldn't that be wonderful?'

'Are we going to their wedding?' he asked hopefully imagining all the tasty morsels of food that would be available.

'Of course we are son. They're coming around on Saturday night. We are going to have a little family get-together. A few neighbours will be here. Uncle Spangler and Auntie Cherry will be coming too.'

At this Michael smiled. Spangler and Cherry Corrigan were always terrific company. Spangler was his father's second cousin who had been brought up in Bermondsey. He was in his early sixties with bright laughing eyes and a mop of fair hair. In addition to a warm personality he could sing with a beautiful voice that seemed to generate happiness. When Spangler came to a party it would always be a good one. He would see to that just by virtue of being there. Cherry was lovely too. Seventeen years younger than Spangler, she was warm in the same way that he was but demure at the same time.

After breakfast Michael made his way to Britannia Street School. Every morning he used to walk past the landmarks that would be etched into the landscape of his childhood memories. From his home in Grenadier Guard Road it would be a trek past the endless rows of terraces, the rooms up and down that contained families in quite crowded conditions. Almost as if it was a symbol separating suburbs from factories, the gasworks rose up like an imposing monolith on the horizon. Beyond this point he would walk past the factories. From outside the ingredients that were used to make the various products could be scented in the air. The throbbing of engines and factory plant could be heard outside on the street. Inside those grim and grey buildings workers toiled in overalls, often in sweatshop conditions for poor pay and twelve hour days.

Michael always took it for granted that one day he would work in one of those places. It never occurred to him that he might have a choice in life to do something completely different from the run of the mill existence it was almost expected he would follow by tradition. Would he work in the first factory that offered him a job? Would he make sauce or would the choice be pork pies, ice cream, rubber tyres, stockings, gabardine macs and heaven knows what else?

Escaping from the industrial area he would walk towards the railway viaduct where trains would rattle across suddenly like thunder before a rainstorm.

There was a construction site nearby. Just what they were building he never knew. Whatever it was during the Blitz it got bombed to blazes and for years afterwards remained a fenced off hole in the ground. Michael had a friend there. He was the night watchman; a friendly man called Bill who always looked tired and drawn in the early morning hours. Bill was an old soldier who had been at Mafeking during the 217-day siege in the Boer War. He would be constantly warming his hands over a coal fire in a steel drum from which charred charcoal embers flickered in the brilliant red of the crackling flames.

Bill would always smile from beneath a cheerful stubble-bearded face. 'Hello son, cold isn't it?' He would always say the same thing. He was probably a lonely man. Michael had a childlike fascination for the way in which he turned a skewer in the fire on the end of which was some chestnuts. 'Would you like one young fellow?'

Michael invariably replied, 'Yes please, Bill,' and he watched as his friend took a mahogany brown chestnut from the coal fire with a pair of tongs. Bill would hand the chestnut to Michael winking pleasantly. And my! – how good those hot chestnuts tasted on a cold winter's morning when he would blow puffs of frozen breath into the air and they would stay hovering like rings of cigarette smoke failing to expire.

He loved going past the bakery shop each morning. The lovely smell of freshly baked bread rose to greet him as he made his way to school. Michael loved to stand outside to absorb the aroma. There in the shop the masters of their trade would roll and knead the dough. They would fold, press and stretch, shaping loaves like a sculptor blending clay into a model. Years later the aroma of bread, cakes and pastry straight out of the bakehouse aroused within him a nostalgia for long ago.

Finally he would arrive at Britannia Street School. Always close by was Bert Greaves the local policeman watching the traffic and guiding the children going to school. He was a reassuring figure on the local streets. Safe, warm, fatherly. If Bert Greaves was around everything was just apples. He was an old time copper though who knew every road and alleyway of his beat. On the surface he was warm and friendly but in fact he was the hardest man on the block not to be underestimated by villains. Many of the local criminals had their collars felt by Bert. After the war he was promoted and served with distinction at Scotland Yard.

Schooldays for many people have often been referred to as the happiest days of their lives. Not so for Michael Forbes. Although there were probably some good moments if he thought back carefully. Years afterwards he could remember times when some of the children in his class used to fall asleep at their desks. This was not through boredom caused by uninspiring teachers. Neither was it from sheer tiredness but through exhaustion. For in the time of the Great Depression and the years of economic hardship afterwards, many of his classmates showed obvious signs of hunger and malnutrition.

There was one school teacher who made a formidable and lasting impression on him. He was a rarity; a radical in an age of conservatism.

Apart from his wonderful usage of the English language he seemed to espouse a message of love and goodwill. Mr Bates was a kindly man with a voice that had a honey-coated timbre about it. Born in the Victorian age he was a Christian who believed strongly in discipline and hard work yet at the same time felt keen to advocate the power of love. He would not have been out of place in the campuses of the flower power Sixties decade. For Michael the lessons of Mr Bates stood the test of time.

One morning, aware that his class were struggling to pay attention to a mathematics lesson, Mr Bates decided to enhance their interest by using the opportunity to speak his own philosophy on life. This would infuse their interest and then they would concentrate on the matter in hand of Pythagoras or algebra.

'I don't appear to have your full attention this morning,' he said looking around at all the girls and boys in the classroom. 'Let me emphasise the value of education. Why do we learn about anything? English, mathematics, science, art. Are these the only subjects we are put on this world to learn about? Life is not just made up of academic subjects. Life is awareness. Life is knowledge. Life is experience. Life is sensitivity.' He strode between the aisles making sure everyone was paying attention. 'We should not go through life with blinkers on only looking in one direction. Life is a learning process. Just because a man is a labourer, a factory hand or a bailer of hay it doesn't mean that he is lacking in intellect or intelligence any less than an Oxford don or a professor of archaeology. We can all improve ourselves by taking an interest in most things.' He stopped to look at the class to check their reaction and then he continued, 'Education is not only about the subjects you learn or being taught to pass examinations. It is about learning principles such as courage, sincerity, honesty, loyalty, love of your fellow human being.' Mr Bates stood at the front of the class allowing a pause for emphasis. 'Love is the most important thing. Learning to love and respect people. If you can grow up with a love of people doing the thoughtful kindly deed, being nice to people, showing kindness and consideration for others, helping someone without seeking reward or favour – if you can grow up doing these things then you have learned to do well. Someone with these qualities has a great strength,' and then Mr Bates added with emphasis, 'A strength to be gentle.'

Those words meant more to Michael than anything else he was ever to learn at school. Maybe in life he was never to achieve the real heights of position and prestige. Perhaps any success he had came from hard work and difficult circumstances that he endured. A student he was never meant to be. Just memorising those words of love and kindness were more beneficial to him than passing any examination.

He was often the one at school who used to bear the brunt of the school bully's aggression. He counteracted this by developing a sense of humour and resilience that never left him. There was no doubt that Michael could not have done without those early tough years. In some ways it was almost an advantage coming from that background. From that sort of upbringing one learns a mixture of toughness and sentimentality that will carry them through all their days no matter how their fortunes rise and fall.

Two

Frank and Honeysuckle may have had little in the way of material goods but in the area of hospitality and goodwill they had limitless generosity. Along with everyone else in Grenadier Guard Road they were hard-up working people. However on the very special occasion of Doris's engagement party it was an open house and everyone in the street was made welcome. They would do their best to look good too. After having a bath in a big tin tub Frank would take some of Honeysuckle's eau de cologne, mix it in with a little bit of olive oil and rub it all over. He would even rub the mixture into his hair and sleek it back shiny and glistening. Then he would put on a pair of trousers with braces, an open-neck shirt and sports jacket. Frank could look a dapper gent when the occasion merited it. He knew how to behave like one too.

Honeysuckle was no slouch at making good with very little either. Her personality and round smiling face were her glowing characteristics. Whatever she wore her warmth and humour shone though. She wore a neat plain dress, typical of that period, for Doris's party. There was never much money in the Forbes' household but Frank and Honeysuckle were skilled in the art of making a little go a long way. Honeysuckle was in her element that day preparing and cutting sandwiches, making pastries, pies and sausage rolls. Michael helped his mother that night while Frank performed the role of barman. He placed bottles of beer, spirits and lemonade together with some glasses around the room. He moved the furniture around creating a space for dancing and pulled out a piano. There would be much fun and music that night.

Slowly but surely the guests started to arrive all indulging in hand shaking, friendly banter and laughter, before the party got into full swing. Then suddenly the door opened and there stood Spangler and Cherry Corrigan with huge smiles on their faces and twinkling mischievous eyes. They were both dressed in the clothes of the Pearly Kings and Queens.

Spangler was an energetic, bouncy man who always seemed to be bursting with fun. At sixty-three he still worked as a painter and decorator. He was Frank's second cousin. Spangler's mother had married an Irish labourer from County Wexford and he seemed to have inherited a touch of the blarney about him. A former boy sailor in the Merchant Navy and a First World War soldier in the trenches, he had also tried his hand as a music hall entertainer before retreating to the safety of a career as a house painter. If ever there was an occasion where a vocalist was required to lead the singing Spangler did not have any inhibitions about volunteering his services.

In contrast to Spangler his wife Cherry seemed demure and ladylike. In fact she was a smiling happy woman of forty-six who had once trod the boards as a dancer and had met Spangler on the stage of the Hackney Empire. Both had been widowed earlier and their infectious enthusiasm for life and sense of humour had brought them together. They adored each other. That was plainly obvious for anyone to see.

Spangler's presence lit up the room. With a fine set of pearly whites his smile was like a light bulb. His constantly smiling face was the butt of many a joke. He could tell them against himself with good humour.

'Spangler! Cherry! How are you?' Frank smiled. He shook hands with Spangler and embraced Cherry. The moment those two entered the room the fun always began. 'Look at those teeth! I don't know how you do it Spangler. If you were a racehorse I'd put money on you every time!'

'Funny you should say that Frank,' Spangler replied, 'when people meet me they're not sure whether to give me a lump of sugar or pat me on my head!'

'And what's with the Pearly King and Queen outfits?' Honeysuckle asked handing them both a glass of their favourite tipple which was stout.

'Well it's an East End party isn't it? And my goodness we know how to have a rip roaring knees-up in these parts don't we?' Spangler said with delight for he knew before long he would probably be the star attraction.

Cherry was quick to make a point. 'We thought with Doris's fiancé coming from Australia we would show him some real hospitality.'

From the corner of the room Michael watched the guests arriving. What a group of real larger than life characters they were. There was Dolly

Mandolino, a big woman in every sense of the word; she was the authentic voice of the East End who had lived there all her life and in her sixties she was a force to be reckoned with. May Maguire also put in an appearance. Uninvited, she came anyway but May had a soft spot for Frank. She had known his own mother and although recently widowed after her husband Alf Maguire had died in prison, Frank discreetly paid her a visit to offer his condolences. May always put a strong value on loyalty and friendship. Bert Greaves also came. Off-duty from the police he was still an East End boy at heart and it seemed strange to those who knew him and May Maguire from opposite sides of the law, that those two could indulge in laughter and happy conversation.

'Well how's my nephew Michael then?' Spangler asked coming through the people beginning to fill the house.

'Fine thanks Uncle Spangler,' he replied cheerfully.

Spangler looked around the room at the smiling guests. 'There'll be some frivolity tonight so don't get embarrassed by the adults here getting into a little bit of the singing and a lot more of the ale sipping. Even your Mum and Dad like a bit of fun now and again.' He winked at Michael mischievously and whispered in a low joking voice casting a backward glance at Frank and Honeysuckle, 'You can tell them off tomorrow morning and send them to bed without any supper!'

Cherry came over to join them. She evoked much feminine warmth. 'He's a good lad young Mike. Just like his Dad.' Spangler and Cherry smiled at Frank. 'Honeysuckle trained him well.'

Frank and Honeysuckle were beaming with pride. Everyone looked happy. May and Dolly, two tough old birds were laughing with the other guests while Spangler looked on at the empty piano just bursting for someone to start playing.

'What do you think then?' Frank said to him. *'Lambeth Walk?'*

'Why not?' He looked across at Cherry. 'Play the piano darling. 'Bout time for a sing song and a dance.'

Cherry moved to the piano. Frank and Honeysuckle struck up a traditional pose ready to lead the dancing. Spangler moved into the centre of the room like a Vaudevillian music hall star topping the bill. Then suddenly Cherry started to play the piano and Spangler began the entertainment as so often he had before. He sang with splendour.

Any time you're Lambeth Way,

Any evening any day,
You'll find us all,
Doin' the Lambeth Walk'

Everyone was joining in the dancing led by Frank and Honeysuckle. Spangler was the ultimate performer who knew just how to work whatever audience he had. The room resonated with happiness and goodwill that night. Michael would never forget that time. Through his youthful eyes he was witnessing happy times that would not come again with his family.

From his vantage point in the corner of the room he watched the party in full swing. The image of it was indelibly stained in his mind like a black and white photograph always to be retained as a treasured childhood memory. It would be all so clear in later years.

Spangler was resplendent in a Pearly King outfit in the centre of the room singing notes with the kind of span Al Jolson would have been proud of but with a London accent clearly obvious. Cherry was at the piano in her Pearly Queen suit, an attractive demure woman, the sort that men would want to protect, yet at the same time hinting an unassuming air of sexuality. Michael would have been embarrassed to admit it but whenever she was around he would retreat into shyness. The local neighbours who had joined the party were working people who Michael saw every day. In the usual course of the day they went to work in overalls while the ladies wore 'pinnies' and scrubbed the doorstep. Now, given the chance to enjoy themselves at a 'hale and hearty' they were as his mother used to say 'well-scrubbed and all done and dusted'. They did enjoy themselves too. Beer was drunk. Pint mugs clinked. Sausage rolls and pastries were devoured. There was laughter and singing and the *Lambeth Walk*.

Frank who normally had a sad appearance was leading the group around dancing. Honeysuckle was really enjoying herself.

Michael smiled at the scene. He was happy to see his Mum and Dad enjoying themselves. For a moment he slipped away from the party and went upstairs to his bedroom. He peered out of the window. Outside it was beginning to rain heavily. Down in the street below he saw a couple dash down the road in the pouring rain. Immediately he recognised his Aunt Doris. Even from the window she looked pretty, sweet and cheerful. He was looking forward to seeing her. There was no show about Doris. She was sincere, serene and calm. Doris was with her fiancé, Jack Hope. Michael caught a brief glance of his handsome glowing face beneath a broad-rimmed Australian countryman's hat. He seemed to tower over Doris by at least a foot. In a few moments Michael would rejoin the party and meet them.

'Can you hear that Jack?' Doris asked. 'That's for us. I do hope you like my family and friends.'

'Geez, I think I'm going to love them!' Jack replied with a laugh in his voice. 'They sound like my kind of people.'

'Let's go in then,' said Doris and she led Jack through the front door as the singing came to an end. Almost as if on cue all of the guests in the Forbes' household turned to face Doris and Jack. Frank and Spangler beamed their street famous smiles and walked across to greet them along with Honeysuckle.

'Doris, darling how are you?' Frank said with a smile hugging his sister. Then with an outspread hand he turned to her companion. 'And you've got to be Jack Hope unless she picked up another one on the way here. I'm Frank Forbes.'

Jack took Frank's hand in a warm handshake. 'It's a real pleasure to meet you Frank. I've heard a lot about you. I hope we can be real mates.'

There was no doubt about that. Although there was almost 13,000 miles between each other geographically from where the other had been born, there was a brash friendliness and direct manner in each other's character they recognised and were quick to warm to.

Honeysuckle moved forward with Michael who had joined them and embraced Doris. 'It's lovely to see you Doris,' then she turned to Jack and greeted him sincerely. 'We are very glad to meet you, Jack. We would like you to feel welcome. You're a long way from home and want you to feel part of the family.'

'I'm really touched,' said Jack who was obviously moved by the little party that had been laid on his behalf. 'You've got good hearts. You really have.' He was about thirty but he had the presence and maturity of a man much older. 'Frank, Honeysuckle, it's good to know you.'

Honeysuckle indicated towards her son proudly. 'We've got a few introductions. This is our boy, Michael.'

'Glad to know you son,' he said shaking Michael's hand with a firm grip. 'I hear you're keen on football?' Michael nodded that he was and smiled. Jack had a strong personality which he felt shy in the shadow of. 'I've been to a few games here. I enjoyed it.'

Spangler and Cherry were eagerly waiting to meet Jack. Frank introduced them. 'This Pearly King and Queen here are my second cousin and his lovely missus. Spangler and Cherry Corrigan.'

'Strewth!' Jack exclaimed looking at their outfits. 'You didn't have to dress up for my benefit!'

Cherry ran an admiring eye over Jack. 'Very, very nice to meet you Mr Hope.' Cherry was impressed. In that part of the world there were not too many six footers with the presence he had. Anyone who was older and wiser would have known Jack was playing the part of the visiting Australian to the hilt. Frank gave him a glass of beer which he savoured for a moment before sinking nearly all the contents in one go. Doris looked at him with an admiring, almost proud expression.

Spangler wasn't to be outdone though. He brought his own style of sparkling humour to the occasion. 'The Forbes family had a distant relative who went out to Australia,' he mentioned as if in passing.

Jack's eyes lit up with interest. 'Really? Was he a migrant?'

'Well in the broadest sense of the word he was,' Spangler's face showed that he was building up for something amusing. 'Frank and I – we're descended from Irish stock. You might say our ancestor was an involuntary migrant. Back in the 19th century there was a bit of a famine in Ireland and he was feeling a trifle bit hungry and felt partial to a pig on a neighbour's farm. Only trouble was, he forgot to tell the neighbour he was stealing the pig and he ended up appearing before the local magistrate. My distant relative was transported to a penal colony in Van Diemen's Land. Hell of a long way to go for a side of bacon rashers!'

Jack grinned happily. He felt at home with these people. Their humour was not unlike those of his own countrymen. 'Well my old man was a pom and I was proud of him. Have you been out there yourself, Spangler?'

'When I was a boy sailor. Back in 1896 would you believe?'

'My word! That was a while ago.'

'Yes. I was on a cargo boat. Docked in every port from Fremantle to Adelaide, Melbourne and at Woolloomooloo in Sydney. It sweltered. Boy was it hot!'

'I believe you've got a farm?' asked Cherry. Everybody was taking a seat now with Jack as the focal point. Honeysuckle was handing out sandwiches and Frank was keeping an eye on everyone's glass but it was easy for anyone to see they were fascinated by this man from Down Under.

Especially Michael who suddenly began to realise there was a much wider world out there to explore.

'Yes it's out in the far west of New South Wales. It's a big place. Sheep, cattle. An orchard. That's when we get rain of course. It's one hell of a dry place where I live. We live in hope of rain most of the time. The station is called Endeavour Downs. The original owner was an admirer of Captain Cook. Hence he named it Endeavour after Cook's ship. My place is the farm and the orchard that I took over when my old man died. Endeavour Downs was virtually next door and after I discussed it with the owners we amalgamated the two places together. It was a good move too. Together we battled our way out of the Great Depression.'

'What's your nearest city?' Frank asked looking keenly interested.

'I'm a long way from any city on the coast.' He took a sip of beer and continued speaking in a slow countryman's voice. 'The nearest major town for me is a place called Broken Hill. It's a big mining town but it's nowhere near as big as the cities on the coast. Sydney is right across the other side of the state. Fine place Sydney. Nice beaches. Trams. People enjoy their life there. I can travel south to Melbourne, Victoria. That's a great city for sport: Horse racing, football, cricket. It's a real big state New South Wales. Takes a lot of getting used to.'

Frank and Honeysuckle were obviously fascinated. Their eyes were shining. 'What brought you over to Kent?' Honeysuckle asked. 'I thought there would be very little in England that would interest someone like you coming from an exciting country like Australia.'

'My late father told me Kent was 'The Garden of England'. He was a market gardener from Eltham. I guess I wanted to get to know my origins. After the hot dry plains of western New South Wales it was a new experience for me. I'll always remember Kent. The hop farms. The oast houses. The windmills. The orchards, green fields and hills and lovely old pubs by streams with boats and barges.'

Frank smiled at the mention of Kent. 'That's where I'm taking Honeysuckle and young Michael here. We're going on our hopping holidays. That's what we Cockneys have in the summer. We go to Yalding to pick hops. The factory closes down for a few weeks and Kent's a lovely place to go.'

'My word it is,' agreed Jack. They both turned around to look at Spangler who had taken up residence at the piano. This was the cue for some good old fashioned entertainment.

'Ladies and gentlemen!' Spangler began as the room fell silent, 'here's a song I used to sing at the old Empire theatres. It's a special occasion. We're here to welcome Doris and Jack. Frank and Honeysuckle have laid on this lovely party for us all – and its been a good one hasn't it folks?'

Almost as if prompted the partygoers applauded and cheered. Frank put his arms around Honeysuckle and Michael. A tear appeared in Doris's eye. She knew there wouldn't be too many more times like this. Not only because she and Jack were soon to leave for Australia but the clouds of war were gathering soon to dramatically change everyone's lives.

'This song is particularly poignant as we're soon to lose Doris and Jack when they set sail for that sunburnt country so far away.' His voice seemed to drop with the emotional thought of their departure in his mind and then he began to sing. Michael would remember the song for the rest of his life.

'Battling Spirits and Kindly Hearts,
They're the salt of the earth.
Cheerful and happy, silent and strong,
They'd give you their heart for all that it's worth.
Old friends and memories,
I will never regret,
It's been a pleasure to know,
So many good people on the way,
Their joy and friendship has shaped the happiness of many a day.
There have been times when my spirits were low,

Because my life wasn't going in the direction I hoped it would go.
But as I journeyed through the years,
New adventures began to unfold,
I took the good with the bad,
And lived a life full of stories untold.
Places I lived in, days gone by,
Were full of characters and personalities as big as the sky.
I remember the old folk and big family gatherings,
Where there were old friends,
Sometimes at lovely white weddings.
For many years I travelled and lived overseas,
But the great joy in returning was in old friends and memories.'

The partygoers cheered and clapped. Then just as quickly Spangler changed the tone of poignancy and started to play a more upbeat tune.

'This one's for you Jack! Get a load of this.' He began to sing a rollicking sea shanty which typified some aspects of Australian character. They were the words of *'Botany Bay'*.

> *'Farewell to old England forever,*
> *Farewell to my old pals as well,*
> *Farewell to the well-known Old Bailey,*
> *Where I once used to be such a swell.'*

Later on in the evening more neighbours and friends dropped by. The home was gradually becoming overrun with people. Frank and Michael sat to one side talking and watching the partygoers. Spangler and Cherry alternated on the piano and the guests laughed and clapped in time with the music. Jack and Doris were enjoying themselves immensely.

'Are we definitely going on a hopping holiday to Kent?' Michael asked turning to him to confirm what he had mentioned earlier.

Frank filled up a glass from a bottle and answered, 'Of course we are, son. Besides money is a bit short. It's always short. And with the factory closed in the summer for a few weeks I've got to keep us all fed. Your Mum loves it too. We'll have a good time, Mick.' Then he said something that really surprised Michael and didn't really seem to fit in with the happy mood of the evening. Perhaps it was the beer he had drunk which was making him feel sentimental. It was as if he wanted to express previously unrevealed feelings. 'I hope I'm a good Dad to you. You know I'd always like to do a lot more for you and your Mum but there's been a Depression. The country is still trying to get itself straight. And now there's talk of war. We'll make this a good holiday.'

Michael smiled at his father. Not for one moment did he doubt that. In another corner of the room Doris and Honeysuckle were engrossed in conversation while Jack mingled happily with the guests. Spangler started to play *'Waltzing Matilda'* and soon Jack was joining in. Doris looked on in delight. It was obvious that she was still learning about Jack. There were always things about him that could surprise.

'We're going to miss you Doris,' Honeysuckle's guard dropped revealing her sadness of Doris's impending departure amid her happiness at gaining a new brother-in-law.

'I'm going to miss you all too,' said Doris. 'When I first took that job on the farm in Kent I felt I'd gone a long way moving from here. I never dreamed I'd become engaged to a man from the other side of the world.'

'Australia though,' Honeysuckle said, almost in frustration at the distance that would separate them. 'It's so far away.'

'I know. Twelve – nearly thirteen thousand miles away by sea,' said Doris. 'But well – you never know – we may all meet up from time to time over the years. You're the only family I've got. I want to keep in touch. What with our folks gone. Out of my four brothers, only Frank came back from the war. And he's never been too well since.'

Honeysuckle looked grim for a moment. 'It was the gas that did it in the trenches. I don't think the air in those factories has been much good for him either.' They both looked across at Frank. 'Well he's enjoying tonight. My goodness he's going to miss you so much.'

They were both feeling emotional when Spangler broke into another tune on the piano. This time he started to sing the *Beer Barrel Polka,* better known as *Roll out the Barrel*, which once started always ensured that everyone else would join in. Spangler was by this time in high party spirits. His eyes were twinkling with mischief and he was determined that everybody should be enjoying themselves as much as he was at that instant.

Jack and Frank stood by the piano clinking beer glasses and singing with Spangler. All the guests old and young sang like there was no tomorrow. The words simply flowed that night. Michael watched from the sidelines. It was a night he would always remember. He studied the faces of his friends and relatives. Then he thought of the song that Spangler had sung earlier. The first line mentioned '*Battling Spirits and Kindly Hearts, They're the Salt of the Earth*'. That's how he would always remember these kind people who had little but cheerfulness and friendship to offer. Somehow that was more than enough.

After they had sung *Roll out the Barrel,* the party began to spill out onto the street. Everybody in the house and street did a '*Knees-up Mother Brown*' as if they would never have a chance to do so again. East End parties are the best in the world, thought Michael. He would never forget that one and he didn't think anyone else who was there that night would either. Sixty years later he would still remember it as if it were yesterday.

Three

It was one Sunday morning when Michael was helping his parents clear out their rooms that he learned more about the Forbes' family history. Frank pulled out from under a bed a huge chest containing lots of old memorabilia. Among these hand-me-downs and bits and pieces he happened to chance upon an old photograph album.

On that particular morning as he studied those old photographs the pages of his ancestry seemed to come alive. There was a picture of an interesting looking character, a merchant seaman with big bushy eyebrows, a hooked nose, laughing eyes and a thatch of premature silver grey hair. He at once recognised the man to be Frank's father, his grandfather Tommy Forbes.

Tommy was an Irishman from Dun Laoghaire who had gone across to Liverpool in the 1880s to find work. There he had signed on as a seaman regularly sailing between Liverpool and the American ports on the eastern seaboard. He soon became familiar with Boston, New York and Richmond, Virginia. In 1885 he was laid off with other ships' crews at one of the London Docks. He sought to make a living as a wharf labourer and the East End became his home.

Soon after Tommy married a local girl called Rose and together they raised four sons and one daughter who became Michael's Aunt Doris. There was a picture of the family taken in the early 1900s that he found in the album. The clothes and hairstyles were of another age when family unity was all important. It was a unity that was shattered with the coming of the First World War. Frank's elder brothers Ron, Harry and Danny were among the first fatalities of that time, all of them dying in the areas that newspaper articles referred to as 'the Front' or 'No-Man's Land'.

Poor Rose was so overcome with grief that she died of a stroke before the Armistice was signed. Frank came back from the war a very sickly man to a life not made any easier by the loss of his closest family.

Tommy Forbes carried on working until his death a few years prior to the outbreak of the Second World War. A strong and happy man he died after a heart attack at work. He had been trying to carry loads that were more than his physical limits.

Michael found it a sad feeling looking through the picture of his father's side of the family considering how their lives had all been cut short by the events that had been thrust upon them. One picture showed all four Forbes brothers in army uniform at the beginning of the Great War together with a very young Doris not more than five-years-old.

On his mother Honeysuckle's side there were many pictures of her own parents Sammy and Sarah Entwistle. Grandfather Sammy was a porter at Covent Garden market. A marvellous photograph of Sammy showed him at work balancing about fifteen baskets on his head.

Grandmother Sarah was a flower seller who was gentle and thoughtful. The Forbes family were not given to churchgoing or private prayer, although Michael gained in faith with the passing of the years but Sarah always thought and acted as he believed Christians did. Sarah believed in helping others; she believed there was no room in life for anger, malice or envy. No wonder she was so serene. That great quality, serenity, shone out of every old sepia photograph of her.

Michael always felt sad that they died before he had fully matured and acquired the wisdom that years of experience bring. He would have so much liked to have been able to talk to them as one adult to another. There was so much they could have taught him. And there were so many things that happened to Michael in later years which would have been of interest and fascination to them.

A short time later the family photograph album was bolstered by pictures of Jack and Doris's wedding. It really was a happy day. It was probably one of the most correct matches in personality ever made for a wedding. Jack was a big hearted man with an easy-going nature, a hard worker and a born man of the land. Doris with her chirpy, cheery nature and sweetness complemented him perfectly. Together they were energetic with a combined strength capable of moving mountains.

It was a fine sunny day when Jack and Doris got married. When they emerged from the church the two of them bubbled with a happiness as golden as the sun that shone so powerfully that day. Jack looked smart in a wedding suit and tie. Doris was radiant and beautiful in her bridal outfit. There is something about a woman on her wedding day. Apart from her natural beauty and the sparkle of the occasion, the inner glow of happiness radiates itself. A woman is never more beautiful than on the day she is married; and so this was the case with Doris.

They were strewn with confetti as they left the church. In the crowd almost everyone who knew the Forbes family was there. Frank and Honeysuckle were at the front of course with Spangler and Cherry close behind. Bert Greaves the local policeman was there in his uniform. The two toughest women in the neighbourhood Dolly Mandolino and May Maguire were there in brightly coloured outfits and big hats. May's four sons, notable roisterers, were dressed smartly and on their best behaviour. There were other neighbours and friends who decided to drop by.

The traditional bouquet of flowers was thrown into the crowd at the church. An eager young girl standing close to Frank and Michael caught the flowers. For some inexplicable reason she turned and smiled at Michael. He felt embarrassed beyond words. This only added to the awkwardness he was already feeling. Michael's hair was greased back Brylcreem-style. He wore a suit with a buttonhole and he thought to himself he would have felt far more comfortable if he had turned up in a pair of his father's working overalls.

After Jack and Doris were married they returned to Kent for a few weeks until it was time for them to sail. On their last night in England they did not have a huge farewell party. At Doris's request they wanted to have a quiet evening reminiscing in memories of days gone by. Frank and Doris talked more about the preceding years than they had ever done so before. They discussed their late parents Tommy and Rose who it was clear they had adored. In a more downbeat area Frank pondered on the lives of his brothers; how the course of life would have taken then had they lived. Then Jack shifted the whole topic of conversation to the future. The theme running through his conversation was that life is for moving on and not dwelling on the past.

It is always an emotional sight, seeing a ship sail away with loved ones aboard. At Tilbury Dock, Frank, Honeysuckle and Michael came to bid farewell to Jack and Doris. For Frank it was as if yet another part of his family was dwindling. Michael had never seen his father cry until then. He was once told 'men don't cry'. What utter rot, he was later to think. A real man is not scared to show his emotions. He was to learn that it is a sign of strength to show emotion, to cry for someone who means the world to them. It is a sign of sensitivity to show love and compassion.

Frank and Honeysuckle hugged Doris in a manner that displayed an air of finality about it. Each shook Jack's hand and then stepped back to wipe the tears from their eyes. Doris hugged Michael and Jack ruffled his hair. They turned and walked up the gangplank.

Smoke spiralled from the funnel of the huge P & O liner that was berthed at the dock. Frank, Honeysuckle and Michael stood together looking up at the decks to where Jack and Doris had ascended. On board the boat many passengers were waving and crying. Streamers were being thrown to and from the various decks of the boat. There was a brass band playing at the quayside which further added to the sensitivity of the moment. Down on the quay the Forbes family stood close together. Honeysuckle was losing her best friend and soulmate. Frank was losing his little sister. Michael was losing his only aunt. They were losing a much loved lady.

The ship's funnels suddenly gave several long blasts. It was at that moment the vessel began to move away. The streamers from the dock to the vessel stretched to breaking point and began to snap. The band at the dockside was playing 'The Wild Colonial Boy' in a wildly enthusiastic manner although it came close to being drowned out by the shouts from the quay and from the passengers on board the ship as it gradually moved further and further out into the river. Frank and Honeysuckle waved for as long as they could. Michael moved forward slightly and stood waving on his own. This really was a prelude to so many changes that would soon occur.

So Jack and Doris sailed away to begin a new life in that far off land which was really just a mystery to the Forbes family of Grenadier Guard Road. To Michael it was just a place in a geography lesson or part of a map that was coloured red and referred to by his school teacher as 'one of the dominions'.

That day as he watched Jack and Doris sail away he felt sad. True. But he also felt good because the next day they were all going on their 'hopping holidays'. That was something he had really been looking forward to. Jack and Doris may have been going to Australia, but he was a happy, young, excited boy going to Kent on the train to pick hops and to him that was a real adventure.

Soon after the departure of Jack and Doris there were times when Michael would walk to the docks near his home and look at the ships that berthed there. He dreamed of the day that he would sail to places like Jamaica, Trinidad and Tobago. But one day he would be boarding a boat for a destination in the opposite direction. That day was to come sooner than expected as war accelerated events beyond everyone's control.

Four

Michael loved the magic of that train ride on the 'hopping special' from Charing Cross to Yalding in Kent. Inside the carriage he sat with his parents together with several cases that contained their bedding. They certainly travelled well prepared. In addition to their pillows and roll-up beds, they took the equipment that they needed for the job of hop picking. Frank had organised a huge tea chest with wheels. This contained essentials covering everything from what they needed for tea breaks to collating the hops. Honeysuckle had carefully compiled a list beforehand of what they were going to need. They took with them; hopping pots, Primus stoves, a couple of wicker baskets, tea mugs, a kettle, cutlery, jam jars and garden scissors.

Outside the view of England was one of an older, slower and less complicated time. Compared to their home in Grenadier Guard Road the view was one of absolute bliss. On each side of the railway track there were lots of rectangular fields, green and gold with a freshly-cut appearance about it. The trees were in full blossom and people were picking apples and pears throwing them into baskets on the ground. In one field there was someone baling hay who stopped to wave to all the Cockney passengers. In another field a horse and plough were making their way. The sky was the kind of pleasant blue that one always associates with childhood summers. Frank and Honeysuckle looked so happy that day.

Michael smiled at his parents. God bless my Mum and Dad, he thought. They were such a hard working couple and their pleasures in life were so simple. This holiday in Kent; the chance to be out in the country with the sun shining down on them meant so much especially for Michael. The days in the hop fields that were coming were to be golden, long, happy and sunny.

Around them the carriage was full of happy Cockneys going on their hopping holidays. There were mums and dads with their children, and grandparents too. They were all sitting there with their belongings looking enthusiastically at the sights of the countryside passing by their window. Somebody at the back of the carriage suddenly shouted out, 'C'mon all you friendly folk! We're on our holidays aren't we! Let's have a sing song!' With smiles all around the man started to sing.

> *'Lambeth you've never seen,*
> *The skies ain't blue,*
> *The grass ain't green,*
> *It hasn't got the Mayfair touch,*
> *But that don't matter very much,*
> *We play the Lambeth way.'*

Before long everyone was joining in. Frank and Honeysuckle started to sing. All the children sang along. It wasn't only their carriage that had echoed into song but the entire train had erupted into verse.

From the opposite track some railway workers smiled at the sight of the hopping special and the refrains of the *'Lambeth Walk'*. They all knew straightaway, of course, the boys from Bow, Stepney, Bethnal Green, Bermondsey and the Elephant & Castle were in the county for the season. The pubs around Yalding and Maidstone would soon be ringing with the tunes of the Pearly Kings. Not all of them though. Some had 'No Hoppers' signs.

The refrains of *'Lambeth Walk'* were heard on the hop fields. It was quite a sight, seeing whole families working and singing together. All of the families and friends grouped around hessian bins really giving the job everything they had. It only took one Cockney family to start to sing and pretty soon everybody else would be joining in. They sang *'Lambeth Walk'* an awful lot that year.

It was a very industrious sight but unlike the plodding discomforts of a steamy factory floor the people were actually enjoying their work. Mums, dads, grandparents, young children and teenagers were all joining in and working hard. Yet all around there was not one single grey face. All Michael could see were smiles and laughter.

Each family worked together. They would strip the hop bushes and build up their tallies in separate bins. Many of the mums wore berets or headscarves that were tied like turbans on their heads. They also wore pinafores, aprons or overalls which by the end of the season had stains from the hops all over. Children climbed up on to the tallymen's carts carrying bushel baskets. The men were more often or not wearing trilby hats, flat caps or hankies tied in a knot on their heads.

There in the sunlight stripped to his shirt sleeves and light trousers Frank was enjoying every minute of it. He was in his element. Never a well man because of his poor chest and appalling cough the sun and the fresh air brought a glow to his face. With the singing in the background and the work in his fingers Frank thought that season there was no nicer way of earning a living.

'Enjoying yourself son?' Frank asked Michael, smiling affectionately.

'Smashing Dad. This is hard work though,' he replied but he really meant it. 'I like it here. The countryside is nice.'

Frank could hardly contain his enthusiasm. 'So do I son. This will do me any time. What about you, Honeysuckle?'

'Oh it's just lovely Frank,' she said in an equally bubbly reply. She pushed her hair back beneath her headscarf. 'Bloomin' hard work mind, but I wish we could do this all the time. You've both got colour in your cheeks.'

'Better than working in a factory,' said Frank. There was a hint of regret in his voice at the prospect of returning to that dreaded place.

Honeysuckle noticed the difference in their complexions. 'I've never seen you both look so well. A bit of sun. Being out in the fresh air and getting some exercise. This has been a real tonic for you Frank.'

Every now and then Michael would pick up a full bag and take it across to the tallyman's cart. Other children were doing the same. He had gone across the field and didn't hear his father's remark.

'Yes this suits me alright,' said Frank. 'Look at the difference in Mike. He's running about and enjoying himself. This is where he belongs. Not in Grenadier Guard Road with little prospect for the future.'

'Oh don't fret Frank,' Honeysuckle chided him. 'We can come here again next year.' She paused, thinking of the possible pending war and added, 'Maybe ...'

Frank looked up apprehensively. 'A very big maybe Honeysuckle my love.'

'Why?' she queried. 'What's there to stop us?'

'Listen, Honeysuckle. It's a beautiful day and we're having a great time but reality beckons. We read the newspapers. We listen to the wireless. It could be war anytime. And then where will we be?'

'Now then Frank. Let's not think about that now. Not here. Not on this golden day in this lovely place.'

'Too true,' agreed Frank, 'and these are golden days. No doubt about it.'

Michael returned from the tallyman's cart and continued to help his parents strip the hops from the bushels. Their hands were covered in black from the juice of the hops. Michael repeatedly wiped his messy hands on a cloth. Honeysuckle noticed his plight and smiled.

'Don't worry about your hands too much Michael, my boy. We've all got grubby hands.'

'It's this juice from the hops. Turns your hands black,' said Frank. 'Get it on your face and you'll be able to sing *'Mammy'!*'

'*Mammy?*' Michael was mystified.

'Al Jolson sings *Mammy*,' Frank said with a smile. 'He was the big singer before Crosby and this new bloke in America. What's his name again Honeysuckle?'

'Oh you mean Sinatra,' she replied.

'That's the one.'

They worked really hard that afternoon. It was fun though for all the families who stripped every hop bushel with furious speed. True to form their hands were black from the resinous juice of the hops. They didn't mind getting their hands dirty. It was an atmosphere that years later Michael would recall; the sight of people singing and working together, and the smell of fresh fields and beer hops that was a taste of a bygone era.

When the pangs of thirst were stirring in the workers the longing for a break for tea, a van drove up and stopped by a wooden shed. From inside emerged a couple of men in flat caps who started to set up tables and urns. A man placed some cakes and kettles on the tables. Thirsty hop workers looked at the tables in keen anticipation. Any second now the cry would go out across the field.

A man in a flat cap and overalls cupped his hands together around his mouth. 'Come and get it you happy hoppers! Tea-O! Tea-O!'

Tea-O! The words still drift down the passage of time. There were probably about 2,000 hoppers right throughout the fields but no more than a couple of hundred where the Forbes family were situated. Tea-O!

That was the sign for everyone to rush up to the tables, fill up their mugs and bring back some cake.

They sat by the hessian bins and drank a well-deserved mug of tea. Even the tea tasted wonderful in the open air. Frank's admiration for this way of life came to the fore once again.

'Ah nice,' he said savouring every drop. 'Nothing like the good old English cuppa. Even on a hot day like this.' He wiped the perspiration from his forehead. 'Wonder if we could make a go of it here sometime. If we left London I mean Honeysuckle. For good.'

'Depending on what happens, Frank. I love the idea of course.' Honeysuckle had spoken as if she only half believed it. The way Frank had spoken though there was more than the hint of possibility.

Frank turned to Michael and suddenly changed the subject. 'Have you ever given any thought to what you want to do when you leave school?'

Michael had thought seriously about his future in the last few weeks. In fact ever since he had watched the boat taking his Aunt Doris and Uncle Jack down the Thames to the world beyond. There were two possibilities going around in his mind.

'I've thought about it. A sailor perhaps on a big liner like the one Aunt Doris sailed on. I wouldn't mind being a train driver either.'

Honeysuckle smiled at him. 'Every boy wants to be one of those at some time in his life. I don't know why.'

'Me too when I was a lad,' remarked Frank. 'Still fancy it at times. What a marvellous life! Going up and down the Great Western or up to Scotland. Now that's a real job.'

'One thing you should know Mike,' Honeysuckle emphasised, 'is that me and your Dad – well we want you to make the most of your life. Whatever you do always remember it's better to try and fail than never to try at all.'

Frank had to add his piece of advice. 'Your Mum's right, son. Have a go. There's a bigger world out there than just factories and our little bit of the world in Grenadier Guard Road. Just because I do what I do it doesn't mean to say that you have to do likewise. I mean my tastes in life are simple. I work where I do because it was a case of a job or no job and I've been unemployed and I don't like the misery of it. I work where I do because I don't know anything else. I'm not trained for anything. Opportunity wasn't a word I heard in our part of the world. Believe me old son, I like this a whole lot better. Give me this hopping any day of the week. This is like a little bit of luxury to me. This is freedom. This really is. The bracts make my fingers bleed and I've got hop juice all over my hands and clothes, and your Mum there is going to have a big bundle of washing and… '

'Don't remind me!' Honeysuckle chortled. She took a bite of cake and handed the rest around.

'So it's up to you,' said Frank. 'When you're the age you are now it's there for the taking.' He finished the contents of his mug of tea. 'Well it's back to work. Let's build up our tally.'

At the end of the day all the families and workers sat on their hessian bins singing some of the old Cockney songs. That, in itself was an entertaining sight seeing so many people of all ages singing together. The toil of the hard work during the day had built up their hunger and with a view to the evening meal in mind sung '*Boiled Beef and Carrots*'. There could not have been many places of work in the world where three generations of families worked, played and sang together.

In among the workers came a couple of local children selling apples and pears, and bunches of dahlias for 'two bob a bunch'. Frank could not resist treating his family. He loved Honeysuckle and Michael dearly but he always felt he had to show it. Beneath his Cockney exterior lay a real romantic who would not have been out of place in a Noel Coward play.

Frank handed Honeysuckle the dahlias. 'For the nicest girl I have ever met.'

Honeysuckle appeared to be a bit embarrassed at first but she gave way to a warm enduring smile of affection and kissed him on the cheek. 'Oooh! You soft hearted old thing.' She meant it too.

'There you go son,' said Frank handing his son an apple. 'Wouldn't it be nice to have orchards nearby and pick them fresh off the tree like this?' It was clear Frank was in his element that day. At the end of the working day they picked up their things and left; a happy family together. With the other hop pickers they walked across orchards, along public footpaths and over stiles and turnstiles. It was a very pleasant walk. On their way to the huts for the hoppers they passed by a thatched cottage with rolled green, velvet lawns. Michael had never in all of his life seen such a place. He could not believe someone actually lived there. It seemed to be a home purely for looking at.

While his parents went on ahead to the wooden huts, Michael dared to stray from the path. His curiosity got the better of him. He climbed up the fence from the side of the path and precariously leaned over the hedge. He studied the cottage and its grounds. The lawns were a lush green carpet almost. The flowers that grew in separate beds around the garden were a blaze of colour; there were red and blue, gold and green mixed in with purples and yellows. It seemed like a wonderland. There were apple trees that hung over the side of the hedge. The apples were a fabulous shiny crimson red; the sort of colour he had never seen on any barrow boy's stand. He gazed at the lovely bronze thatch that spread over the huge roof of the cottage. It was a picture-book sight, a postcard portrait and then a little girl appeared on the lawn. She at once caught sight of him. Instead of being alarmed she waved mischievously at him. He waved back nervously and then got down from the hedge.

Michael was thirteen but her cheeky wave had put stars in his eyes. He smiled to himself at the thought of her. Quickly he ran along the path across to the common where the huts were. On the common all the hoppers had congregated outside their makeshift accommodation. These buildings looked very stark and bare in contrast to the attractiveness of the lush green Kent countryside with its oast houses and mixed colours from the blossoms of trees and plants. To Michael on that day standing outside one of those huts and absorbing everything in view was like being in a little bit of heaven.

The early evenings after a long day picking hops were always a nice time. All of the hop workers would sit down in front of their huts with wood fires burning. Above the fires stew pots would be cooking with the evening meal. The fires crackled and sparked in the mauve darkness and the wood smoke rose in silver-grey spirals against the night. What a magical sight! Even the scent of it would evoke nostalgic thoughts in years to come; a blend of burning wood and charcoal intermingled with the aroma of stews and vegetables cooking.

Honeysuckle cooked, as she always did, a beautiful tasty stew. The family had worked so hard during the day that they ate their meal vociferously. The food tasted so good that Michael would end up scraping the plate until it was almost clean. It was a long and exhausting day, and a yawn would quickly follow.

In the intervening hours between the evening meal and bedtime it was a most convivial period. Families would talk. People would chat idly. New friends would be made. The children would play either with each other or their mums and dads. Sometimes the elderly people would go for a stroll arm in arm, in those beautiful hours of twilight. On those pleasant nights Frank and Honeysuckle were content just to sit on the grass looking into the night and absorbing the lovely night air. It was as if Frank had found his peace in that place.

Michael felt enormously reassured by the calm look on his face. His eyes were normally streaked red and he had a permanently tired expression. It was probably due to the fact that his poor chest precipitated a cough that would sometimes trouble him in the night time hours. Very rarely did he ever get a full night's sleep. Here though, in the countryside it was as if a new peace had found his soul. He and Honeysuckle sat in a splendid silence enjoying that simple joy of being close to someone you love dearly and for whom words are not necessary. Just being there was security in itself.

Inside the hut the bedding for all the hop workers was laid out on the floor. Everyone was well and truly ready for a good night's sleep. Michael settled down to the strange comfort of a hut floor bed and he looked around at the other people. For the first time in his life he found himself making a character study. Compared to the fresh-faced, clear-eyed country people of Kent, his fellow Londoners showed in every nuance and crevice of their features, the toughness of their upbringing. They were fine people. Good-hearted, cheerful, outgoing, hard working people, who found joy in the simplest of life's pleasures.

One thing they all had in common was the fact that they were battling spirits and kindly hearts. Engrained in their faces were the features of people who are poor but are all of good spirit and generous heart. They stubbed out their cigarettes, took a last minute sip of a hot drink, tucked their children in, kissed goodnight, and rolled over to make themselves comfortable for the hours ahead.

In the half-light Michael looked at his parents. Honeysuckle was already fast asleep. It had been a long hard day for her. Not only had she picked the hops and cooked the meal but in addition had hand washed some of their clothes. He studied the look on his father's face. What was he thinking? Was it a look of tiredness or sadness? There was very little to distinguish between either expression where Frank was concerned. He turned to look at Michael and broke out into a friendly grin.

'Another long day tomorrow. Best get a good night's sleep.' He lay back and prepared himself for sleep. 'Goodnight, son,' he added in a quiet and soft voice.

'Goodnight, Dad,' Michael said and rolled over. He thought of the pretty girl in the cottage. He smiled to himself at the thought of her. Then he closed his eyes. A moment later the lights went out in the hut. He had a long, peaceful sleep. It was only the beams of early morning sunlight streaming through the windows that woke him early the next day. He was so eager to get back to work he was the first to rise in the hut.

Five

While his parents were working in the fields he could not resist the opportunity to go back and take another look at the thatched cottage. Michael climbed up and stared over the hedge at this wonderful house which he was sure belonged in a dream. He kept hoping to see the little girl who had waved. In his wildest fantasy he imagined returning to this place in years to come as an adult with all the flamboyance of a prince who would surely meet this young girl, when she would be a ravishing young woman; the princess of his dreams. Naturally they would fall madly in love and get married. And of course they would live in this wonderful house.

Michael's fantasy was just accelerating nicely when the young girl's mother and father stepped out onto the lush green-rolled lawns. He got down quickly and peered from behind a bush. Above him were hanging some beautiful golden apples. The temptation was far too much for him. After about fifteen seconds of resisting the forbidden fruit he reached out and plucked a mouth-watering apple. He bit into the luscious surface of that delicious fruit and drooled over its succulent flavour.

'You're not scrumping my Dad's apples are you? He'll go bonkers if you are!'

Michael turned around in alarm at the sound of a girl's voice. On the public footpath he found himself facing the little girl who lived in the cottage. He was beside himself with embarrassment. He was awed by the girl who was blonde and had all the signs of growing into a beautiful woman. Noticing that Michael was blushing red she smiled warmly at him which only served to unnerve him even more.

'I – I – I'm sorry,' he stammered. Michael thought that he must have sounded like he was really bumbling with his speech. She laughed at his nervousness. 'I've never seen a lawn as green as that before,' Michael added quickly.

'You were the one who looked over the hedge yesterday,' she pointed out.

'Yes – yes,' he stammered once more. 'I'm sorry. I haven't seen a house like that before. Not where I come from.'

'You're from the East End aren't you?' she asked.

He felt more relaxed now. 'Yes I am,' Michael said proudly. 'I'm here with my Mum and Dad. We're on our hopping holidays.'

'Are they working in the fields over there?'

'Yes, I'm just going to join them now.' He paused. Michael felt a twinge of shame for helping himself to a piece of her father's fruit. 'Sorry I took one of your apples.'

She looked at him sympathetically. Then surprisingly she stepped up and shook the tree so that apples fell all over the place. Michael looked on in amazement.

'I don't suppose my Dad would mind much really. He told me you all work hard here because you haven't got much where you live. Are your family poor?' The girl looked at Michael innocently as she posed the question.

Michael appeared uneasy at the question. 'Well we haven't got much if that's what you mean. But nobody I know has got much either. I never really thought about it. Everyone in our neighbourhood seems the same to be honest. My Dad works in a factory. What does your Dad do?'

'Oh he's an engineering draughtsman,' she replied matter-of-factly.

'What's a draughtsman?' Michael enquired.

'Oh he works with plans and drawings. A bit complicated.' The girl smiled at Michael. It was a warm smile that uneased a boy still getting used to the attraction of the opposite sex. Like Eve in the Garden of Eden she handed Michael some apples. 'Go on. Take them all and give them to your people.'

He was surprised at her generosity. 'Gosh, thanks.' He grabbed as many apples as he could carry. Then he thought perhaps there should be some introductions. 'What's your name?'

'Margaret.' She enquired as to his. 'What's yours?'

'Michael Forbes. Thanks Margaret. That's very nice of you. My Mum and Dad will really love these.' He looked at her admiringly. He was not quite sure how to do so but he wanted to impress her. 'You're very nice.'

Margaret looked at him a bit perplexed but once again she smiled at him in a manner that stirred him. When she grew up it would develop into the kind of smile that would melt men's hearts. She shrugged her shoulders. 'Oh well I'd better go now. I suppose you'd better go back.'

'Yes we've get lots of hops to pick. Your house is really nice. I don't ever see places like that in London. I'll go and join my Mum and Dad now. Thanks for the apples.' He walked a few steps and then turned back to look at her. She was watching him walk away. He added a final farewell. 'Bye, Margaret.'

'Bye,' said Margaret. She seemed quite emotionless. For a moment she looked across the fields to the hop pickers. They were all frantically busy but happy. Margaret entered into the gate of her house. However as she turned into her garden she looked back with interest. Under her breath she said, 'Bye, Michael.'

He returned to the fields where his Mum and Dad were working. He must have looked immensely pleased with himself as he carried a huge bundle of apples. Honeysuckle stopped and elbowed Frank. 'Now where did you get those from?' Honeysuckle asked with a wary eye.

A look of alarm crossed Frank's face. 'Oh my goodness! You haven't been nicking apples have you young Michael?'

'Margaret gave them to me,' he said beaming proudly. Frank was a bit surprised and eyed Honeysuckle with disbelief.

'Margaret! Who's Margaret when she's at home?'

'She lives in the cottage over there.' Michael pointed to it. His mother could hardly believe her ears. 'She gave me all these apples from her garden.'

'She lives in the cottage?' Honeysuckle repeated. 'Whatever have you been up to? Our sort don't mingle with people of their ilk.'

Michael was a bit alarmed at their anguish. 'I wasn't doing anything. I was just hanging over the hedge … '

'Hanging over the hedge!' gasped Frank. 'Oh my goodness! What were you up to?'

'Yes, I was looking at the house. And she came up behind me, and asked me what I was doing. I said I was looking at the house because where we come from there are no places like that. Anyway she gave me the apples.'

Frank's expression changed. 'Well I brought you up to be honest.' He was firm now but not stern. 'Are you telling me the truth? You didn't scrump them apples did you?'

'I am telling the truth,' Michael insisted. He felt slightly hurt that his Dad doubted him.

Frank smiled. 'That's alright then.' With a wink he tapped Michael on the shoulder. 'Give your Mum and Dad one each. Take a couple for yourself. Now take the rest and give them to as many people as you can.' He added an afterthought. 'Always share when there are others around you that have got very little too. Remember that old son. Do you hear?'

'Okay Dad,' Michael replied. He handed his parents an apple each and then he walked around the field handing the rest to the other hop workers. When he returned his mother was looking at Frank with deep affection. 'Always share when there are others around you that have got very little too. Nice words, Frank.' She beamed at him with adoration.

They were nice words. That was the kind of people the Forbes were. They might not have had a halfpenny between each of them to scratch their backsides with but whatever they had it would be shared with people less well off.

***

The Forbes family went into Maidstone from Yalding a few times that season. Michael liked that town very much. Compared to his part of London it seemed to be fresh, clean and an ideal place for anyone to live. He was to grow up to like places where there was a comparative ease about the lifestyle and all the facilities of a town were available. This seemed to sum up Maidstone back in those days. When Frank got paid at the end of the first week the family sat at the top of a green double decker bus travelling through the town. Flush with money after having been paid, the three of them felt like royalty. Frank bought them the biggest ice creams he could buy.

'We did well. Didn't we?' Honeysuckle was thrilled at the amount they had earned.

'Why?' Michael asked rather naively.

Frank could not have answered the question more quickly enough. 'Why? We had the highest tally! That's why! We worked hard. Tea breaks 'n' all. I feel flipping proud. We all pitched in on our little patch in the hop fields and to come top … Very nice indeed. So is the cash we made too.'

'And if that isn't enough, guess what else Michael?' Honeysuckle asked.
Their enthusiasm knew no bounds. 'Oh no. What Mum?'

'You know the hoppers are having an end of season party?' said
Honeysuckle. 'Did you know a few people are going to do a turn?'

'No,' Michael replied.

His mother announced smartly, 'I talked your Dad into having a go!'
This really surprised Michael. 'What are you going to do Dad?'

'I had a natter to some people and I thought I'd recite a really wonderful
set of lines with a little bit of accompaniment from one of the lads on the
harmonica.'

'What's the name of it Dad?' Michael asked with a mixture of eagerness
and curiosity.

'It's called *Because we're Cockneys*. It's a good old down-to-earth
monologue from the music halls.'

Well this was news to Michael. Frank had a touch of the music hall
artiste in him.

On that same day they took out an open rowing boat for a leisurely
time along the river. There were plenty of other boats on the river, some
of which had an expensive aura about them. The family were in a jovial
mood that day. Michael rowed while his Mum and Dad relaxed and
looked around at the houses and boats along the river. Even though his
Aunt Doris had been away for a few weeks Michael was thinking about
her. It was almost as if his Mum and Dad could read his mind for her
name suddenly came up in conversation.

'I wonder how Doris is getting on,' Honeysuckle said. Michael slowed
up on rowing. He let the paddles dip and splash gently.

Frank contemplated his answer. 'I expect Doris is enjoying the boat
trip I imagine.'

'Where's Aunt Doris now?' Michael asked. He knew the boat trip took
several weeks to Australia and the route encompassed many exotic ports.

'Well it takes about six weeks by boat to Australia,' said Honeysuckle.
'She's been gone several weeks now. Another week or so and she'll be there.'

Frank turned to Honeysuckle and looked at her face for signs. 'Do
you envy her?' he asked her quietly.

Honeysuckle looked up at the clear sky for a moment. But it wasn't
the sky she was looking at. It was the horizon. Michael was sure that
she, like Frank, secretly yearned for a new life, perhaps in the County of

Kent or an area not too dissimilar. Even further afield. Australia had been hitherto unknown to her but the prospect seemed intoxicating.

'I envy her the excitement. The thrill of starting something new. Something different. Wiping the slate clean and going forward.' There was a real sincerity about the way she spoke. 'Don't get me wrong, Frank. It's not that I don't appreciate all your effort for us. I do and on days like this I think it's just wonderful. But when I think of the chance Doris has to go somewhere else where she can forge a new life without any hangovers from the past, well I think it's an opportunity to change her life. Do you know what I mean?'

'I know, love,' answered Frank putting his arm around her.

Michael continued to swish the oar against the water on that lovely afternoon. For some reason he began to think that all their lives were going to change. From the way his parents had spoken it seemed to him that the seeds of change had been well and truly sown by the departure of Aunt Doris.

Far away on the other side of the world Jack and Doris were on board a P & O liner within sight of Australia. The new life that Honeysuckle and Frank had talked about was about to begin for Doris.

Six

On board the liner the coast of Western Australia came into view. Jack had been eagerly looking forward to seeing the coastline of his homeland once again. After several years working on English farms he was going home to the land he believed was the best country in the world. For Doris this was one of the most thrilling days of her life. From the deck of the ship she gazed out at this hot, vast, brown land that was to become her new home.

The whole voyage had been a real adventure for Doris. When the ship had left Tilbury Dock it had sailed out of the Thames into a new world. The ship had sailed past Shoebury, the North Foreland and down the coast passing the White Cliffs of Dover, then out into the English Channel and across to the Bay of Biscay. The ports of call from then on were the sort of places that it seemed only the very rich would be privileged to visit. For Doris it was nothing short of miraculous to travel there. Marseilles and Naples were the first places outside England she had ever travelled to. In Naples Jack and Doris roamed the bustling streets, visited the ruins of Pompeii and had a meal of pasta in a café at a vineyard. It was her first taste of Europe and she thrilled to the sounds of different languages on their home ground.

Port Said in Egypt was her next stop. Doris and Jack stood at the ship's rail late at night and watched some Egyptians coming on board carrying bags of coal on their head for refuelling. Each man chanted as he strode up the gangplank. Grenadier Guard Road shrank into the past very quickly. From Port Said the ship sailed through the Suez Canal where the shimmering sands of the desert stretched out on either side. Occasionally in the far-off distance through the heat haze the lone figure of a camel rider could be seen. The heat rose up from the golden desert sands and mingled with the scent of date palms. There was a stillness about the desert, broken only by the sound of the liner easing itself through the locks of the canal. Then it was out into the Red Sea and they were greeted by the sight of Arab dhows drifting across the crystal waters.

The ship sailed on to Aden followed by a stop at the gateway to India, the bustling city of Bombay and then down to Colombo in Ceylon. It was there Jack and Doris had a meal at the Mount Lavinia Hotel in Hill Street, Colombo and went for a swim in the sparkling blue waters that lapped against the golden sands of Paradise Beach. Truly these were adventures and places Doris never dreamed she would ever experience. How wonderful it all was for her.

A further stop in Rangoon, Burma opened up new horizons. Doris and Jack looked on in wonder at the sights of the Sule and Shwedagon pagodas as well as the colourful local populace that seemed to incorporate many Buddhist monks. Then it was on to Penang and Singapore, a place still containing aspects of British colonialism as well as elements of a pre-war Far Eastern city yet to change its complexion in the modern world. Raffles Hotel in Orchard Road oozed affluence and history of another age. To Doris the Long Bar of Raffles was light years away from the Saturday night jostle at the British Grenadier pub in the East End. Doris had travelled on a once-in-a-lifetime journey and had seen the sights and sounds of places she never dreamed that would ever figure in her life. People from her working class background did not go to places like this. At least this was what she thought.

The weather was hot and sultry on the day that Doris saw Australia for the first time. All the passengers looked out from the decks at the north-western Cape of Australia. Most of the travellers aboard wore light summer clothes. They eagerly studied the thin strip of coastline in the distance. The first view on the horizon line appeared to be a continuous length of golden-brown land above which was the deepest and fullest blue sky that many of the English people aboard had ever seen. There was a band on the very top deck of the ship which played '*Waltzing Matilda*' in a very rousing jazz-orientated manner.

Sunglasses and sunhats were the order of the day for all passengers. From within the crowd of eager onlookers Jack and Doris emerged to view the coastline. After several sun drenched weeks they both looked very tanned and fit. Doris particularly looked good that day. The sun had tanned her English skin a beautiful colour of copper-gold.

'Do you know what that scent is in the air blowing across from the coast?' asked Jack. Doris smiled and nodded that she did not have a clue. 'It's eucalyptus, darling. That's what it is. The scent of that tells me it's home. This is your new home, Doris.'

'I can't believe we've come so far,' said Doris. 'It's like a dream. When I think of all the places we stopped at after we sailed out of Tilbury. Marseilles, Naples, Port Said. Egypt! I was so excited when we went through the Suez Canal and the Red Sea and then on to Aden, Bombay, Colombo, Rangoon. I don't mean to sound as if I'm gushing but now I'm looking at Australia and I still can't believe it.'

Jack who had been secretly worried about taking Doris so far away was delighted at her new found enthusiasm. He turned to face her. Doris's eyes were shining with excitement. This was the moment to keep the pot bubbling.

'The best is yet to come,' Jack promised her. 'This is a young country and its been through the Depression like England and the United States but it's a good country. We'll stop over in Sydney for a few days. It's a big smoke. Not like London though. It's real good. It's a waterside city and I'll show you some really clean golden beaches like Avalon and Dee Why and Whale Beach. We can take a ferry boat ride to Manly. I'll show you the Harbour Bridge and Watson's Bay and Kings Cross. If you want to buy anything there's a big department store called Anthony Horderns you might want to look around. If you want a night out we could go dancing at the Trocadero. We could shoot through on a tram to Bondi. You've never seen surf until you've seen Bondi.'

Doris thought for a moment that there were traits in Jack's manner of speaking that were similar to her brother Frank. She wondered if in Jack she had found not only a husband and lover but a friend and confidant.

'Sounds like we might need more than a few days there Jack, if we're going to do all that. I'll treat it as a holiday before we head for the bush.'

'Might be right at that sweetheart. Anyway how do you feel? I sensed the closeness you have with your family. I thought Frank was a good-hearted man and Honeysuckle was just lovely. Their boy Michael was a little shy but he seemed like a good kid. You've got a warm hearted family.'

'I'm too excited at the moment to miss anything Jack. But I know I will. Then again I'm your wife and this is where my life is now. I want it to be a good life for both of us.'

'With determination – and dare I say, probably a lot of hard endurance

I reckon we'll have a good life.' Jack was a blatantly honest man. 'I've got the feeling you're going to find it very, very tough going at first. It'll be hotter and more desolate than you've ever known. Rougher and brasher too. I can promise you though it will be different and exciting. It'll take a lot of getting used to you know.'

Doris too was as honest as the day was long. 'I realise that Jack. I don't expect green fields like England where we're going. I didn't marry you under any misconceptions about what the future is going to hold. Don't worry though, Jack. I take my marriage vows very seriously. Where I come from if a marriage doesn't work out, the brothers come round to find out why. I'll stick by you no matter what. No matter how rough.'

'I'm a lucky man aren't I?' said Jack squeezing her. He was thrilled that he had apparently struck gold with Doris. Not only was she a warm and attractive woman but she would be a determinedly faithful and loyal wife. 'Well Doris there it is. Western Australia. Any first impressions of the coastline?'

'Y'know Jack,' Doris considered the view, 'It looks big, hot, brash and …'

'Yes, sweetheart.' Jack listened eagerly. 'That's a pretty good description.'

'It looks like something from out of the Wild West,' she stated. 'I half expect to see John Wayne or Clark Gable riding by.'

At this point a middle-aged Australian moved alongside them and looked over the rail. He glanced at them. He appeared to be moist eyed at the sight of land.

'Good to see that rugged passionate land again.' The man took a few breaths of the air. 'Smell that eucalyptus in the air?'

'I can,' Jack emphasised. 'It's new though to my good lady wife here. She's fresh out of England. Have you been away for a while?'

The man was an affable sort with an easy going manner about him. 'Yes, too long I think. I've been teaching in English schools for quite a few years now but what with the growing friction in Europe I thought it was time to go home and sit on the backyard verandah for a while and take in the mulga (shrub). I've missed it.'

'Are you going to the shipboard concert tonight?' Doris asked the man.

'Am I going?' he bubbled. 'Oh my word I am! In fact I'm in it. I guess I have always had a touch of the theatrical in me, and I thought tonight I'd try out a poem I've just written. I'm hoping to get it published you see when I get home to Perth. Thought I would give it a go on the ship's audience. If they are moved then I'll know I am on a winner. If they're not impressed I'll just go away and have a quiet drink on my own.'

'Well we'll have a beer with you, win or lose. Won't we Doris?' Jack emphasised.

'Certainly,' answered Doris. She was puzzled by the man's interest in poetry. 'I didn't know Australians had a feel for poetry. I thought they were an outdoor race not interested in books.'

The man smiled at Doris's assumption. 'You couldn't be more wrong. Australians are next only to the British for their love of poetry. Bush poetry mainly. It must be the Celtic influence in us from our forebears. We've had many famous poets in our history. I could name you quite a few: Will Ogilvie, Breaker Morant, Henry Lawson, Dorothea Mackellar, Banjo Patterson.'

Jack introduced himself. 'Well I'm Jack Hope and this is my wife Doris.'

The man shook both their hands. 'I'm very pleased to meet you both. My name's Ben Daneman. From Fremantle originally but my relatives live in Subiaco in Perth.'

'We'll watch out for you tonight then Ben,' said Jack.

'Has your poem got a title, Mr Daneman?' asked Doris.

Ben appeared to be thinking deeply and then he broke into a smile. '*Australia, My Rugged Passionate Land.*'

'That's an interesting title,' remarked Jack.

'There will be a few homesick people on the boat,' said Ben. 'There will also be a lot of people new to the place. It might stir the blood in their souls.'

'You've certainly got me interested,' Jack assured him. 'We Australians have got a reputation for being happy-go-lucky free living larrikins but I reckon as people we've got a lot of sentiment and sensitivity about us. It's something the rest of the world doesn't see in us. By God, we Aussies appreciate our land.'

'We're a nation of romantic wanderers, Jack,' said Ben in a knowledgeable manner and here he spoke with a degree of authority, for Australian history was his favourite subject. 'From Gallipoli to the Somme. It's the scent of eucalyptus and stringybark that always brings us back. Mention a billabong and a gum tree, a swaggie on a bush track, the name of a marsupial and it'll bring tears to the eyes of any Aussie a long way from home.'

Jack and Doris looked forward to the ship's concert that night. Far, far away and getting further to a new life every day, Doris felt really excited and interested in Australia and Australians. Much of the concern that night at sea centred about English people on board making imitations of show business acts that could have come straight from the provincial music halls and repertory theatres at home. Even the ship's entertainment officer and compere of the concert was a jovial North of England fellow. He stood at a microphone in front of the audience of passengers and introduced each act. Finally he came to the point where he introduced Ben Daneman's contribution to the evening.

'Ladies and gentlemen,' the compere boomed in an entertaining style. 'We've seen many interesting acts tonight. Singing, dancing, comedy, ventriloquism. I think we've got more talent here on board ship than they have on the stage in London's West End! Mind you. I don't get to the West End too often in my job. But if Wilson, Keppel and Betty; Al Bowlly, Bud Flanagan and good old Billy Cotton and his glorious band are looking for some support acts they need look no further than this fair vessel.' He clasped his hands together. 'Right! The next act is something a little bit different. I said we had talent of all kinds. This is a poetry reading with a difference. I know many of you good Australian folk are a little bit homesick and looking forward to landfall. Many of you others are first-time visitors to this beautiful country. Now here's a man who'll bring a tear to your eye and a thrill to the spirit with his rendition of a poem that he wrote which is dedicated to the homeland he loves so much. Ladies and gentlemen, would you kind people be so good as to put your hands together and give a magnificent welcome to a school teacher who has been teaching in schools up and down the British Isles. He is now on his way home to Perth, Western Australia. Let's hear it passengers and friends for Mr Ben Daneman!'

The audience applauded as Ben Daneman walked to the microphone. Ben shook the compere's hand and bathed in the spotlight of the moment. In the audience Jack and Doris watched Ben eagerly. He was an Australian of the old-school projecting sincerity, warmth and character in every timbre of his voice.

'Thank you very much indeed everybody,' said Ben in a wonderful voice that commanded respect. 'It has been a long sea voyage and the pull of home is like a magnet to us all. I hope the words of this poem will be a reminder to us all what a fine place we come from, and what a fine land the newcomers are going to for the first time. Ladies and gentlemen, this is a poem about our land: *Australia My Rugged Passionate Land*.'

Doris turned to Jack and whispered, 'I've been looking forward to hearing this.' No sooner had she mentioned these words than Ben started to speak in a rich voice that summed up visual images in the mind from his poetic lines.

'Beneath a territorian sky there lays an ice white cattle skull
upon a scorched red plain,
Where the sun bears down with furious might, scant regard,
and there is no sight of rain,
This dusty colourful terrain is home to Jackaroo and Overlander,
Miner and Prospector and maybe even you,
Of bronze red earth, drained out river beds, gleaming white ghost gums
spreadeagling against a sky of rich deep amethyst blue,
It is a land of characters, legends, trails blazed, fortunes won and lost,
experiences gained and still to come,
Away from the roar of chaotic traffic, crowds of city people,
commitments and work that is humdrum,
Beyond the realms of my imagination, my suburban lifestyle,
my heart remains a bushman's and a roamer of a time gone by,
And every now and then, more often now, I cast my memory back to my
youthful territorian days when above me the parakeets used to fly.
I was younger then and rode the great bush tracks beneath the Southern
     Cross in all of my youthful glory,
With only a blanket roll and billy-can I lay gazing at the stars glittering like
     crystal chandeliers over this land which is an untold story,
And there amidst the purple shaded blackness of the outback sky as crackling
     campfire embers smouldered sparkling into the air,
It came to me how young a land we were and how in less than two hundred
     years with anvil, forge and physical might we have become a land so fair,
I thought of it all night long 'till the morning came and the mischievous
     sunlight twinkled twixt amongst the treetops taunting me.
The red sun rose upon a golden horizon line where once it was only the
     people of the Dreamtime who dwelt so quietly.
Back in 1788 eleven vessels of the First Fleet came from far away off English
     shores to found a great new colony where everyone could be equal from
     deckhand to ship's commander,
So the ships sailed in; the Sirius, Supply, Lady Penrhyn, Charlotte, Scarboro,

Friendship, Prince of Wales, Fishburn, Golden Grove, Barradale and the
    Alexander.
Toil and tears, pain and hardship produced the very backbone of our nation,
Give it the strength and resolve transforming it from convict settlement to
    a land for battling people to decide their ultimate lifetime destination.
This rugged passionate land of flame red gorges, coral reefs, mountain ranges,
glassy lakes and good solid earth,
Became a place of flourishing townships, settlements, fine cities; Sydney,
    Brisbane, Melbourne, Adelaide, Hobart and Perth.
We became a nation, not just a colony with a race of people who showed
    initiative and endeavour in every field,
Our land produced heroes and heroines, sportsmen and statesmen, battlers,
    doctors and enterprise, our future was sealed.
Peter Dawson sang the popular song, Dame Nellie Melba's operatic
    renditions
Thrilled us with her clarity of voice,
During the Depression years Don Bradman scored century after century
    upon the cricket pitch giving sport lovers reason to rejoice,
We exported wool, beef and all types of mineral, our troops were at the
    Somme, Beersheba and Gallipoli,
Yet our land thrived on challenge, our wrinkled suntanned countenance
    evolved from adversity
Our story was told by different poets and writers; Henry Lawson, Banjo
    Patterson, Dorothea McKellar and Marcus Clarke, C.J. Dennis wrote
    ' The Sentimental Bloke', Steele Rudd 'On Our Selection'
Classics of Australian life in shades of light and dark,
The Anzac Digger and the surf lifesaver, the mother rearing children, the
    country fellow, cattleman and city gent.
They all built this land of which I'm justly proud and to which my patriotic
    love will be ever sent.
The land is Australia from which I've been away too long and where I'm
    returning to,
I love its splendid grandeur, its harshness and its beauty, and the thrill of
    seeing once more its sky so blue.
My Australia, Your Australia but to me it will always be
Australia my rugged passionate land.'

Ben stepped back from the microphone and at the conclusion of his poem the ship's passengers gave him a rapturous applause. Jack turned to look at Doris. He smiled at her expression realising Doris's enthusiasm had been fired by the words of Ben Daneman's poem.

Seven

While Doris and Jack were in the final stages of their journey the Forbes family were coming to the end of the hop picking season. This holiday that they had enjoyed so very much really had been a time of joy. It was a time in Michael's memory that he would recall for being the weight on the scales of history that tilted from those last precious days of peace to the frantic years when the world was at war.

Michael was young but even he could see why everyone enjoyed themselves so much at the hoppers' farewell party. The time between peace and war was narrowing. It was as if every family knew this was the occasion to enjoy their friends and relatives while they had opportunity to do so.

In the hut that night a real rip-roaring party took place. There was a tremendous singsong with everyone joining in practically raising the roof. Many of the people drank beer or their own special mixtures from jam jars as there were few glasses available. Quite a few people put on acts that night. There were impersonations of prominent showbusiness figures of the time; people like Max Miller, Tommy Trinder and Max Wall. Then it came to Frank's moment to do a turn.

To a big round of applause from the hop workers who were by now considerably warmed up, Frank strolled to the centre of the hut. He was wearing a flat cap, an open-neck shirt, trousers with braces and his face was full of expression and mirth. His eyes twinkled. He sported a huge grin. Frank was well in the mood for the occasion. Behind him came Jack Faley, one of the hoppers who was going to play the mouth-organ as a musical accompaniment to his monologue.

Frank began his act like a music hall artist. 'Ladies and gentlemen! Fellow hoppers! Fellow hoppees! And most of all my fellow Cockneys!!' At this everyone in the hut went wild, stamping their feet and cheering loudly. He spurred them on. 'Louder, folks! Louder!' Michael felt they were heard in Dover, let alone Maidstone! 'Tonight,' continued Frank, 'I shall give you a little recitation of a monologue. This jolly gent behind me is Mr Jack Faley from the Elephant and Castle.' The audience applauded. 'But before I monologolise – if that's the right word for it, but who cares anyway, I'm going to sing an old time tune and I want you to sing along.' He turned to Mr Faley and doffed his cap. 'Let's be having you then. *'If you were the only girl in the world''* Frank began to sing the words of the song as Mr Faley played his mouth-organ.

Everybody joined in as Frank sang and it was a moving sight as the sound rose to a crescendo with a spontaneous round of applause immediately following on. Almost as quickly as the applause died away there was a hush so quiet it was deathly. Then Frank, who was master of the moment, signalled to Mr Faley to play a note so he could commence the monologue. Frank was in his absolute element that night. He rendered the words of the monologue using expressions and hand gestures and raising his voice from high to low. For such a down-to-earth nice man Frank surprisingly had the power to hold his audience in a spellbound manner. In another life he could have been a variety star easily at home on the stages of the Hackney or Chiswick Empire theatres.

It was a strange irony that as Doris was on a liner on the other side of the world listening to poetry at a shipboard concert, almost at exactly the same moment in Kent another audience were listening to Frank deliver his monologue.

> *'I'm not a squire of the shire with a mansion and some grounds,*
> *I'm just an ordinary fellow whose friendship knows no bounds.*
> *I'm not a wealthy man from 'Up West' with a team of horses*
> *and a sailboat or a yacht,*
> *I come from London's East End and I don't pretend to be something that I'm not,*
> *My friends, do you know why?!'*

Almost spontaneously and in a very loud manner everyone in the hut yelled out, 'Why?' Frank continued with the audience in the palm of his hand.

> *'Because I'm a Cockney and I'm blooming proud of it!*
> *Because I'll not make a concession to pretention,*
> *Or false dimension to condescension.*

Now I ain't a toff from Mayfair,
Neither am I an Xavier from Belgravia,
And I was always taught to play fair,
In whatever I have to do,
Or try to do,
And maybe you too do the same.
Now a lot of us who are there today have never known what it's like to be
*   rich,*
But through times of struggle, our East End hearts and spirits will take us
*   through all of this.*
You will see us at King George Docks, Petticoat Lane, Bermondsey and
*   Canning Town.*
Cheerful, hardworking with good humour as the day is long, from morning
*   to sundown.*
Because we're Cockneys!
On the day that I was born the Bow Bells rang – they nearly deafened me,
My dear old Mother – God bless her heart – she advised me wisdomly,
Go forth my son, do your best, be of good heart, enthusiasm is the name of
*   the game,*
Never feel sorry for yourself when things don't work out the way they should
*   because, my friend, its apathy that makes you lame.*
Yes my friend we're Cockneys!
And we're proud of it, and we're a cheerful, chirpy, perky bunch who will
*   always have a go.*
So remember that, my friend, wherever you may go.'

Stanley Holloway, Frank was not. The lyrics William Shakespeare would have scoffed at. But this dialogue, with only a harmonica backing, scored a huge hit with the hop pickers that night. They applauded wildly and cheered. Then while everyone was in the height of a party mood Mr Faley took his harmonica and started to play the *'Hokey-Cokey'*. Soon everybody was dancing and singing together. It was an extremely happy ending to what was unknowingly the last holiday the Forbes family would ever have together. In the next few weeks their world, as with everybody else's, would change dramatically.

It was very hard to go home the next day. There had been a warm, comforting feeling about Kent. It was hard to say whether it had been the happy atmosphere they had all lived in or if it had just been the fact that Kent looked so glorious that year and truly lived up to its reputation as the Garden of England. That was a time of unity among people, a time of friendship and love. The nostalgia for that time would ache in Michael over fifty years later.

When the Forbes family arrived at Grenadier Guard Road it was late at night. There were no real glad feelings at being home again. Each of them carried their belongings, and bedding, and wheeled the tea chest along the road. The wheels squeaked on an otherwise noiseless night. Compared to the open fields of Kent, Grenadier Guard Road seemed very dark and unwelcoming. The sadness of being home for Frank was evident in his eyes. It was as if in the space of the journey all of his original tiredness had returned. The tiredness was not just a mixture of weariness from age combined with the sleepiness of a long train journey. It was the symptoms of a man tired with his lot in life, tired of the day-to-day struggle, and tired of the frustration of not being able to achieve his full potential in life.

Honeysuckle was very observant of Frank's wavering moods. She gripped his arm with a feeling of reassurance and put her other arm around Michael. There they stood, the three of them at the front of their home. It was too much of an anti-climax coming home after such a happy time that they simply did not know what to say at the thought of resuming their normal day to day lives again. Michael looked at both his Mum and Dad's faces and realised just what they were thinking. He was growing up fast and his perception prompted him to say something.

In a very quiet voice he said, 'It's been a smashing holiday, Dad.'

Frank replied almost immediately in an equally hushed voice. 'You're blooming right it has Mick. It's been the best.'

A faint smile appeared on Honeysuckle's face. She immediately took charge of the situation. 'This is where we live unless I'm mistaken. I think a cup of tea wouldn't go astray would it?' She looked at her husband and son in a jovial manner reminding them of the man in the flat cap who set up the urns on the hop fields and she cried out, 'Tea-O!'

They laughed at the thought of the memory. Tea. The great prompter compelled them to pick up their belongings and enter the house at Grenadier Guard Road.

It was early on Sunday morning when Michael rose from his bed. He went to the window and looked out at the old familiar view. He peered out at a very drab, empty desolate street; a street that one day he would be homesick for. It was very, very quiet apart from the sound of a dog barking in the distance. While he was dressing he could hear his parents talking in the kitchen. Normally he did not listen to his parents in their private conversation but he was still revelling in the memories of the hop season and wondered if they were discussing it. Michael took a peek through the space between the door and listened with interest.

Honeysuckle and Frank were sitting at the kitchen table with a pot of tea and were involved in conversation. Frank was in a soul-baring mood trying to get much off his mind while Honeysuckle, as always, listened attentively and kindly.

'Coming back here is so hard, Honeysuckle. I wish we could have gone on for ever there. I didn't half enjoy it, luv. Both you and Mick were well. I enjoyed myself.'

'I know you did!' Honeysuckle said with emphasis. 'The last night party was just wonderful. You virtually stole the show.'

Michael heard Frank laugh at the thought of it. 'Yes, that was wonderful wasn't it?' he said and then his voice changed in a most dramatic manner. 'But now it's back to hardened reality isn't it eh? Back to the factory and the sweatshop. Trying hard to make ends meet. Worrying about the future all the time especially about how young Mick is going to make his way in the world. I really would like him to do well in life.'

Honeysuckle was concerned. 'You're not alone on that Frank. He's a good lad. But the world's changing. I mean the way people are talking. We could all be at war soon. Then all of our lives are going to change. Whether we like it or not.'

'That's what worries me,' said Frank in a voice that betrayed his utter dismay at the pending situation. 'How on earth are we going to handle another fiasco like that last one? It makes me cry, it really does. For four years I fought it out as a youngster in the trenches in France and Belgium. I watched men die alongside me. I saw my friends go down in the blood-soaked mud as hails of bullets came flying at us from all sides. The scent of death still haunts me. I got gassed for my trouble. Wrecked my health in the process. I lost three brothers. Ron at Flanders. Harry at Ypres. Danny at Passchendaele. I saw explosions, men dying in agony. Then after going through all that – fighting for what we hope is going to be a better world, a lot of us come back to face hardship and struggle. The toffs roll in cash. The working classes have got empty pockets and patches in their trousers.

And we've been through it all haven't we? The General Strike. The Great Depression. Factories with appalling conditions or else no work at all. If that's not enough we have had to battle for decent lodgings. Even a reasonable place to live in has been hard to come by; living in places with rats and bugs, fleas and peeling paint! And! And no damn flaming chance of anything better. We struggle with barely enough money to live on. Don't you feel you just want to give it all away and start somewhere else? Kent never looked so good from where we are at this moment.'

There followed a terrible silence during which time Michael realised just what an enormous battle life had been for his father. Honeysuckle spoke up in her continuously supportive and kind reassuring manner. Michael felt so grateful from the confines of his room that his mother could ease the obvious mental agony and frustration his father was enduring.

'You're hurting yourself, Frank. You don't hear me complaining do you?'

'You never complain Honeysuckle and I love you all the more for it.'

'There then. What are you worrying about?'

'What am I worrying about?' Frank asked, his voice showing more signs of control now. 'It upsets me I haven't been able to do better by you and Michael. I feel so helpless. I feel like I've failed you both. You both deserve something much better and it's beyond my abilities to give you the best in your lives.'

Honeysuckle reached out and squeezed his hand. She began to speak with a quiet restrained firmness but there was not a sign of temperament in her voice. It was calming, controlled and gentle.

'Frank, listen to me. We are people just caught up in the times that we live in. It's not your fault that this is where we live or that we do what we do. We're just – just battlers and that's all there is to it. We're battlers, working people. That's not a bad thing to be, is it? We've got our pride. We're decent people. We don't do anyone any harm. And do you know what else, Frank? I wouldn't change any of it. Looking back with all our struggles, our whole way of life has had more true value to it than any toff in Belgravia or Mayfair would ever realise.'

Frank's expression showed genuine interest in her opinion. 'Why? I don't understand.'

'Because there's real love in this house, Frank. That's why. The three of us pull together, no matter what. And that's something to be proud of isn't it? I've got a husband in you who cares deeply for me and our son, and I wouldn't swap you Frank for royalty or the paltry crown jewels. I couldn't put a price on the love that exists between us. It's to be valued far more than any material possessions in the world. There are some families I know round here and you know them too, where they argue and fight all the time at home. Then when they've finished they go and fight with a gang on the street somewhere, and it starts to spill over. There's a bloke down the road whose wife is going round the bend slowly and they've got thirteen kids in two rooms. Frank, we've got an awful lot to be thankful for. My word we have. And I've never asked for more than what we have together. Anything more would be a bonus.'

There was another silence for a moment. Frank gazed at Honeysuckle in a look that suggested a mixture of embarrassment and sadness. Michael continued to look through the crack in the door at them. He found himself smiling at his mother's compassion and her direct manner.

Frank smiled slightly at her and said, 'Well I s'pose we'd better have our breakfast then and get through the rest of our lives.'

'We'll always get through,' said Honeysuckle defiantly. 'We're made to survive. That's our very nature. That's the way of the people round here. Maybe we'll never live in luxury. That's not the point of life is it? The point is to survive. As long as there is a meal on the table, a comfortable bed to sleep on, and there's food in the larder, and we're warm and we can have a laugh. That's all that really matters.'

'I think you're right love,' Frank said quietly. 'But it doesn't mean to say that we can't think and hope for better things. If we could start again in Kent. Wouldn't that just be lovely? Or maybe even if all goes well for Doris we could – well, make a new start.'

Honeysuckle was startled. She interjected. 'What do you mean? A new start?'

'Yeah. That's right,' replied Frank. 'I was thinking if it all went well for Doris and Jack, perhaps we could all give it a try out there.'

'What? Out there in Australia? What brought this on?' Not only was Honeysuckle stunned but so too was Michael. 'What…at our ages? In our forties!'

Frank explained. 'I think it was that night Doris brought Jack round. I liked his manner of looking at things. He was open and direct and a good companion. I liked his humour and the way he talked about Australia. He obviously loved his country. He loved his work and his whole way of life. And I know he loves Doris as deeply as I love you. I mean he really feels good about everything. I like the open air. I like working in the country. I felt good doing what I was in Kent. Every day there I felt good about life. Do you know what I mean?'

'I know exactly what you mean Frank. But – but Australia! It's a bit different than catching the hopping special to Yalding in Kent isn't it? It's so far away. A real upheaval!'

'Do you know something, Honeysuckle? I've got this dream.'

'A dream? What are you on about?' Honeysuckle was bewildered.

'This dream of mine?' Frank bared his soul and inner feelings in a way Michael had never heard before. 'This dream. It's for all of us. It's called happiness. Where we've been living all these years we need to have our dreams about how much better life can be for us all. I get the feeling sometimes that because we live here, it's almost expected of us that an unwritten rule says that we shouldn't even dare to be different. An invisible voice is saying 'Oi, who do you think you are then? This is your life and you've got to accept your lot without asking questions'. Why should it be? Why should we just take what life doles out to us? Why shouldn't we try for something better? Not only for us. But for Michael most of all? Don't get me wrong. I love this country. But I hate the way by virtue of us being so-called working class, we're bracketed in this spot that says we have to live in poverty. I want something better for you and Mike.'

'You have really, absolutely stunned me,' said Honeysuckle. 'I have never heard you talk like this before. I didn't know you harboured such deep feelings. Maybe there is a way out of all this.'

'I never wanted much in life, Honeysuckle. But it's when I think of you and our lad. You both deserve better. I've always been a working man and although it hurts to admit it, I'll probably always be one. Maybe my wage is never going to get that much higher. If there's overtime and shifts though, God knows, I'll work all the hours under the sun to fend for you and Mick. It's where we live. It's what we're missing. We can do better for ourselves. I know that. I want a better way of life for us all.'

'So?' Honeysuckle asked very seriously. 'It's Australia you have in mind? Or perhaps Kent?'

'Yes,' replied Frank very definitely. 'But look, just bear in mind what we've been talking about. We won't talk about it for a couple of months. Then I'll ask you again and we won't think about it. Whatever you decide we'll go right out and do it. Will you think about it very seriously?'

'Okay, I'll do that Frank,' Honeysuckle answered.

At this point Michael closed the bedroom door. He sat on his bed for a while pondering to himself about what he had just heard. Finally after thinking about the prospect of a new life in Kent or Australia, he took out his school atlas and thumbed through the pages. He studied a map of Australia and considered the size of the country in relation to Russia and Europe. It seemed to be a huge country and soon his Aunt Doris and Uncle Jack would be travelling across it to a place called Endeavour Downs Station somewhere in the vast Outback.

Eight

It was a couple of weeks later that Doris and Jack sat on a train travelling through the bush of New South Wales. Sydney had been a welcome honeymoon spot for Doris. On the voyage the boat had stopped at Fremantle for Perth, Adelaide and Melbourne before sailing under the great span of the Sydney Harbour Bridge one hot and glorious morning.

While in Sydney they had done all the things that Jack had promised. They stayed at a little bed and breakfast hotel in Darlinghurst from which in Jack's words they 'shot through on a Bondi tram'. There on that golden beach they luxuriated in the sun and the surf. They took a ferry from Circular Quay to the North Shore beach of Manly and in the evenings they danced to the big bands at the Trocadero. Sometimes during the day they would walk hand in hand in Hyde Park or the Domain and the Botanical Gardens. Other times they would sit in Martin Place and watch the people passing by. They were both happy to be in each other's company.

Doris did not make the mistake of allowing herself to be lulled into a false sense of security where she would imagine that living in the bush would be a similar lifestyle to that of an Australian coastal city. She was far too perceptive for that. However the scenery she viewed from the carriage window as the train moved across the desert came as a bit of a shock to her even though she had mentally prepared herself.

The scenery was a huge unending view of barrenness and desolation. It was a mixture of orange-brown and red dust set against the depths of a vivid blue sky. The only striking features on the horizon line were the occasional luminous ghost gum, baobab or jacaranda tree. Life seemed very remote too. Sometimes a goanna would scamper across the scrub. It was a lizard which in miniature had an almost dragon-like appearance about it and seemed to snare its tongue at the passing train. Across the desert the train rolled along like one of the old-time American freight trains travelling across Indian country giving rise to Doris's early observation that the coastline was like something out of the Wild West.

Inside the train Jack was fast asleep. His broad-rimmed hat slipped down over his head covering most of his face. He was sitting with his trouser braces loose, a shirt un-buttoned to his stomach, and the sleeves rolled up above the elbow. Jack's head was perspiring in beads. It was very, very hot inside the carriage and red dust from the desert outside flared up and covered the passengers.

Doris sat opposite Jack. She wore light cotton clothes to keep herself cool but she felt the heat tremendously that day. Is this what she would face every day from now on? While Jack slept Doris looked out at the stark desolation of the bush with apprehension. She wondered for one terrible moment just what she had let herself in for. Outside in the wilderness despite the blistering, shimmering heat, it looked icily inhospitable. The sight frightened Doris far more than she could have ever imagined. How could she cope?

Worriedly, Doris shifted her gaze to a few other passengers within the carriage. There were a couple of jackaroos who sat close by. They were big, broad and muscular in appearance, and wore huge rimmed hats and heavily sweat-stained vests. The two men were loud voiced and raucous, and had deep bellied laughs that were blood curdling. A few seats away sat an Aboriginal station worker who mumbled to himself in some sort of incomprehensible tone. In another seat in the carriage sat a woman who was not so much fat, but gross and overburdened with blubber. Doris stared at her in awe. The woman too was struggling with the heat and she continually ran a perspiration-soaked handkerchief over her head and chest. For a moment Doris stared and suddenly caught the woman's eye. Doris half-smiled to avoid the glare from the woman. She quickly averted her gaze to another passenger. This time she found herself looking at an elderly man who had the signs of skin cancer apparent about him. The man was suntanned golden brown with dark blotches from the type of consistent sunburn experienced by Australian countrymen of the bush. Oh God! It all seemed so harsh! There was a potent sense of terror within Doris. She could not make her mind up whether the view inside the carriage was worse than the one outside. Again she looked out of the window and her eyes froze at the sight of white gum trees on the red desert.

Further up the railway line three men anxiously waited at Endeavour Downs railway station. It was not so much a train station as barely a single platform and siding with a long roof for protection from the sun. One man walked up the length of the platform and gazed into the distance for signs of an oncoming train. He checked his watch and looked back at the two others who also waited impatiently. The man who constantly checked his watch was Roy Lane, the station manager at Endeavour Downs. Roy was a man in his forties who typified many of the finest qualities of Australians who worked in the bush: warmth, decency, toughness and integrity. He was clad in typical countryman's clothes: broad hat, safari shirt and khaki trousers. Roy was the kind of man who could automatically assume the mantle of leadership without seeking it. He was capable of handling any crisis by applying a good common sense attitude at all times.

Behind Roy on the platform the two other men wore clothes of a similar fashion. One was Freddie Bannan and the other was Johnny McCullough. Freddie was a man of good humour, a hearty laugh and disposition who could always be relied upon to add some mirth to even the gravest of situations. He too was in his forties.

The final member of the trio was a grey-haired Scotsman. Johnny McCullough was fast approaching fifty. He had a lived-in face and at first meeting appeared to be a somewhat dour man but this was in fact a mask that concealed a person of great depth. In truth, Johnny was a poetic Celt with a sharp intellect and a colourful personality.

Roy turned around and called out to his friends, 'The 1.15 is late as usual.'

Freddie grinned and tilted back his hat. 'Only three hours. It was four last week.'

'Are you sure Jack and his wife are going to be on this one?' asked Johnny.

Roy walked back towards them and the shade of the platform roof. 'His telegram from Sydney said. See you Wednesday. Stop. It's your shout Freddie. Stop.'

Freddie laughed to himself. 'Yeah. That'd be right. Don't see the bloke for a few years and he's asking me to line up the drinks already!'

Johnny was the first to see the spiral of dust rising into the air. 'Better put your hands in your pocket now Freddie. I can see the train coming.'

In the far-off distance the train came travelling through the shimmering haze rising from the railway line. It took a while to finally come into view. The three men on the platform waited anxiously to see their good mate and his new wife.

On board the train Doris and Jack started putting their belongings together. Doris and Jack stared out of the window without saying anything. Eventually the train approached the station. For Doris it felt more like the day of reckoning had come.

Down on the platform, Freddie, Roy and Johnny stood in breathless expectation not saying anything. The doors of the train remained closed for what seemed ages but was actually for only a minute or two. Roy glanced at Freddie as if to suggest that Jack and Doris were not on this train. They were about to leave when one of the carriage doors swung open. They watched with curiosity as a couple of suitcases were put down onto the platform. From within came the foot of a lady. Then Doris emerged. She stood on the platform looking about her. Doris was like peaches and cream to the eyes of the men. Her English rose looks stood out like a flower in the desert.

Freddie turned and whispered one word to Johnny. 'Strewth!' He looked at Doris admiringly from his safe distance. Doris was a picture of gentleness in her brash surroundings. Freddie was lost for words. Then after a pause he said, 'If she's not an English lady then I'm a Scotsman.'

'No, I'm the Scotsman!' Johnny retorted quickly and dryly.

Jack suddenly stepped down from the train carriage and stood on the platform with his arm around Doris. He had a huge smile on his face from ear to ear and he was simply glowing with happiness at the sight of his friends. The men started to walk towards Jack, happy to see him.

'Got those beers ready Freddie?' Jack said in his quiet laconic style.

'What d'ya mean, it's my shout?' Freddie replied sharply. 'I stood you your farewell drinks. What's up with you?' They embraced and shook hands. 'How are you, you old devil? You don't deserve to look so good mate! Half your luck eh?'

'Good to see you too, mate.' Jack was genuinely pleased to see each of them and he shook their hands and embraced them. 'Roy, Johnny, I know I'm home when I see you fellows.'

'Welcome back Jackie, old mate. We've missed you,' said Roy.

'The place hasn't changed a bit,' Johnny reassured him.

'That's good to know,' Jack said gratefully. Then he gently pulled

Doris around. She had been feeling a little shy and hesitant about meeting Jack's friends. 'Fellows I want you to meet my wife, Doris.'

Doris smiled dazzlingly at them. The effect she had on each of them was spontaneous. The men as a matter of courtesy pinched the rims of their hats except in the case of Johnny who removed his hat completely and lightly shook her hand.

Jack introduced his friends to Doris. 'Let me introduce you, Doris. These three larrikins are some of the best mates any bloke would wish to have.' Then he became the old laconic joker again. 'But that's enough buttering up of them. You want to see their bad side!' He indicated towards Roy. 'Doris this is the best station manager in the district, Roy Lane.'

'Welcome to Australia Doris,' Roy said in a warm and affable manner.

'Thank you very much Mr Lane,' replied Doris. She was quite oblivious to the fact that her Englishness and unassuming attractiveness had entranced the three men from Endeavour Downs.

'I hope you'll settle in well,' said Roy. 'My own wife Josie has been looking forward to you coming. She's been hankering after another lady to talk to. I think she misses out on some good old woman talk.'

Yet another wave of alarm triggered off shock waves in Doris's mind. It was reflective in her voice. 'How many women are there altogether?'

'Just – just you and Josie – at this stage.' Roy spoke with surprise as if he had already expected Doris to know this. Doris gave Jack a glance of some apprehension. 'Could be a few more in time though.' But even he didn't sound too sure and added as an afterthought, 'Hopefully.'

Jack quickly moved on. 'This bloke here knows it all when it comes to the land, cattle, sheep, orchard growing. He knows the lot. He's a very hard worker too. Not bad for a one-time bank clerk from the city. This is Freddie Bannan.'

Freddie took off his hat. 'I guess if I was to say to you a bit different from London that would be something of an understatement wouldn't it? So I will simply say one word Doris. Welcome.'

'That's the nicest word anyone could be greeted with,' Doris answered, clearly impressed by the genuineness of the man.

'Finally,' said Jack, 'this bloke here is from your part of the world.'

Johnny grinned broadly. 'What d'ya mean Jackie? I'm no' a Sassenach. I'm from bonnie Scotland.'

Jack continued with a smile on his face. 'This is our resident station carpenter and odd job man, Johnny McCullough. He's a bit of an all-rounder. Old sea dog, bushie and character too.'

'A great pleasure to meet you Mrs Hope,' Johnny said in an accent that had more than a hint of his Glaswegian upbringing in its tones.

'And you Mr McCullough,' smiled Doris.

Freddie reached down and picked up Doris's suitcases. 'Now that Jack's told you all the bad things about us why don't we head out to your new home at Endeavour Downs? The truck's outside. Prepare yourself for one hell of a ride.'

'Let's go then lady and fellow larrikins,' said Roy.

With great reluctance Doris left the shade of the platform roof and headed out into the searing heat. All five of them entered a truck and within a few minutes Freddie was driving towards Endeavour Downs. Freddie drove fearlessly in the bush. Little wonder this vehicle was probably the only one for a hundred miles anyway, it seemed. Red dust spun into the air from beneath the wheels of the truck leaving a cloud streaming behind its path. They drove well off the beaten track, far away from the railway line and a long way from what passed for roads in the Outback. Around them the scenery was changing fast from being a constant mixture of yellow-red and orange sand, gum and wattle trees to land where cattle started to appear interspersed at infrequent intervals. Gradually the cattle started to increase in small numbers until it became apparent that this was a huge herd.

Doris looked at the scene in a curious and anticipative sense. Jack on the other side of the vehicle was delighted to be home and he felt relaxed and happy to be there.

'Endeavour Downs. Isn't it beaut?' Freddie boomed. Doris was speechless. 'Big too. This is only the beginning of it!'

Doris tried desperately to look happy. In her mind she was trying hard to work out how she would fit in here. This was a man's world she was going to try and adapt to.

'My piece of land is only a small part of this though.' Jack was so excited at being home, he could hardly wait to get back. Doris knew that she must try as hard as she was able to make a life here. It was going to take a tremendous amount of effort, goodwill and patience. But as Doris had told Jack, she took her marriage vows very seriously and would stick by him no matter what.

The truck drove through a clump of trees and there was the scene of the Outback men in the work they lived and breathed in these parts.

The magical sight of jackaroos riding on fine strong horses rose up to greet them in the flurry of strong sunbeams glowing on rising dust flying up from beneath the hooves of the cattle as stock whips cracked. It was a stunning sight when viewed for the first time by an outsider like Doris. She would always remember the noise of the herd, the sounds of the drovers shouting and the whips striking at the ground. It created a hypnotic initial effect. Dust swirled creating a hazy appearance.

Hardly had Doris taken in this astonishing scene then in front of the truck was an everlasting plateau with a number of white huts and buildings. A tall Artesian well with a rotary mechanism was the highest landmark on the horizon. Nearby were some orchards which seemed to be full of bloom even in a harsh climate like this which obviously did not favour agriculture. There were some sheep paddocks and some plots of land cordoned off by separate fences. The sound of the truck brought out a few people from the front of the largest house.

Jack turned to Doris. 'This is it love. This is your new home.'

'This is – this is it? Gosh.' Doris was hesitant but cautious in not giving away her true feelings of fear about the future. 'I think you're right, Jack. This is going to be different for me – and exciting.'

Roy added another note of welcome. 'And to welcome you Doris, Josie's preparing something pretty special for you. A good old Aussie get-together.'

Doris smiled happily although her inner self realised that it would take a lot of adjusting to this harsh new way of life.

The 'get-together' as Roy had described it was in fact a sizzling barbecue on an Outback night which was clear and full of stars. There were about twenty people there. They were nearly all local men from around the district, mainly station hands from nearby properties. Jack and Doris were the centre of attention that night. They walked around shaking hands with everybody. After a while it seemed that once the formal introductions were over the men mingled together and talked about things common to them. Doris still felt uneasy and she looked across to the verandah where Roy's wife Josie was sitting alone.

Josie was a pleasant country woman who was aged in her middle to late thirties. She was golden haired but wrinkly, tanned and weary looking. Obviously the years of living in the bush had taken their toll on her. Doris picked up a glass of beer and walked over to Josie who was also sipping the same.

'Hello Josie,' said Doris. 'We haven't had much chance to speak. Mind if I join you?'

Josie looked delighted. 'Sit yourself down and have a yarn. I've been looking forward to the chance to talk to another woman. I've been up here surrounded by so many fellas I reckon I've even begun to think like one.'

Doris sat down beside her. 'Jack's having a bit of a reunion with the boys by the look of things. I'll let him catch up with his friends.'

Josie examined the look in Doris's eyes. She was very intuitive. Josie recognised at once fear, anxiety and curiosity. 'I know how you feel Doris,' Josie said knowingly. 'It's all a bit strange at first isn't it? The bush and the dust. The heat. Even the people. Pretty brash and overbearing on first sight. Course I'm a city girl myself too. When I married Roy I was fresh out of Adelaide. Lovely town you know.'

'I know. The boat stopped there for a day. I went with Jack on a tram to a beach at Glenelg. I liked it a lot. Clean streets and shops too.'

'Yes. Nice place,' Josie said with a reflective smile. 'I was a young girl of eighteen when I met Roy. I had a lot of dreams like many young girls of course. Good man. Good home. White wedding. Kids. The whole box of dice. I met Roy at a dance at Woodville Town Hall. He seemed so strong and quietly confident. He rattled like a Bendigo tram about the bush and I just fell for him. The way I saw it the bush offered a different life than just living in the Adelaide suburbs. I was not wrong!'

'No regrets surely Josie?' Doris asked fearing the worst.

'Oh none at all Doris. What I'm saying is it was pretty hard for me, a girl from Adelaide coming out here. Even harder for you coming out here all the way from England. I know it's going to be really hard for you. You're probably a bit afraid now. Aren't you?' Josie paused to check Doris's face for signs. 'Am I right Doris?'

Doris glanced around nervously. Then with recognition of the warm tones in Josie's voice she turned and looked at her realising she had made a new found friend. 'I think I'm going to get on well with you Josie. You understand perfectly how I feel.'

Josie tossed her head back and laughed. 'That's alright Doris. Kindred spirits you and I will be. My boy Terry – he's going on twelve – takes up a bit of my time what with his schooling 'n' all but if you ever want to talk woman to woman I'm here if you need me.'

'Thanks, Josie. I think I'm going to need some support,' Doris said with a smile.

'There's something about the bush you know Doris, that gets into your soul after a while. When you sit on the verandah at night and you see the stars stretch across and the night sky is clear there's a peace and there's a silence, a quiet where you can hear your own heartbeat. It's the hot, big land stretching out before you. It's the hot stillness of the day. The scent of the gum trees and the early morning sun rising and the kookaburras in the sky. It might be the shimmering haze in the distance when the bush is sweltering in the summer heat. Oh yes Doris, you've got it all to come. I envy you in a way.'

'Why's that Josie?' Doris was curious.

'When I came up with Roy from Adelaide I was young and excited. Gosh, it was a thrill. That first golden time.' Josie raised her beer glass with Doris's. 'Well here's to you Dot. Good on you. Happiness always.'

Doris clinked her beer glass with Josie's. 'Cheers and good health.' For the first time that day she felt more at ease with herself and less anxious about the future. Doris knew that at least she had one soulmate to confide in.

Nine

Spangler looked at his watch. He had been waiting in The British Grenadier pub for Frank to show up. Together that night they were going to have a rare evening out to see Max Miller at the Empire Theatre. He was sitting chatting amiably to Dolly Mandolino and May Maguire. All the customers in the pub were dressed up that day. The reason for it was that one of the local villains, Joe Lucky was being buried that day. He had recently succumbed to a heart attack and that afternoon there was to be a New Orleans type procession through the streets to bid him farewell.

'I remember Joe Lucky from the old days,' said May sipping a gin and tonic. 'Always a gentleman. No matter whatever he may have done.'

'Made his money on the racecourses – he and his boys of course,' Dolly pointed out and turning to Spangler who was gulping a shandy she asked, 'Did you ever have a bet through him?'

'Not on your life Dolly,' he replied with a smile. 'My old man once told me never put anything on a horse except your backside.'

'Sounds good advice to me,' said May glancing at her watch. 'Well it's two o'clock. The funeral procession should just be drawing up about now.'

Almost as soon as May had said that the customers started leaving the pub to go outside. Spangler, May and Dolly made their way out to join the others lining Grenadier Road. Frank, Honeysuckle and Cherry were there already. They greeted each other and watched as the procession came into view. Children, dogs and onlookers joined in.

'Blimey, he didn't do things by halves did he?' gasped Frank.

A team of horses pulling Joe Lucky's coffin in a carriage appeared. Immediately behind a group of jazz musicians in dark suits walked down the street playing a traditional number. Close behind came close relatives, members of his gang and other local villains like Louis Malone and Fuzzy Davies followed on. Espying Dolly and May, Louis Malone raised his hat and grinned at them. He looked like a younger version of Errol Flynn and oozed conceit.

'Cocky sod that Louis Malone,' May retorted. 'I used to slap his arse when he was young. Look at him now. Thinks he's cock of the walk.'

'His mother Vera was a saint, mind you,' said Dolly. 'Died when he was about eight. His dad went soon after that.'

The jazz musicians went into a rousing number which seemed to act as a trigger for everyone else to walk behind. The small group of Frank, Honeysuckle, Spangler, Cherry, May and Dolly stayed behind.

'Not joining in then May?' asked Frank. 'Your Alf and Joe were pretty thick once.' Barking dogs joined the procession, as did little children with their mothers.

'Thick as thieves you mean, Frank?' she answered. 'No, it never brought my Alf any happiness. He died in prison you remember. No, I've left those days behind. There's nothing heroic about villainy. Just grief and prison visits. No more misery for me and my boys thank you.'

'You know where we are if you need us,' added Frank.

'You've got a good one there, Honeysuckle,' May said with a smile. 'Where are you all going? You're dressed up like a rich dog's dinner.'

'We're off to see good old Maxie Miller at the Empire,' Honeysuckle said with enthusiasm.

'My word we are,' said Cherry. 'We'd better enjoy ourselves before the war comes.'

'War!' May repeated with a touch of scorn. 'Cobblers to that! I'm still going to enjoy my gin at the British Grenadier whatever happens. Eh Dolly?'

'Too right 'n' all my girl,' Dolly agreed.

The Empire Theatre was crowded that night. Max Miller was always a big draw card with his risqué sense of humour and outlandish costumes. The moment he walked on stage his very appearance and twinkling personality seemed to liven up the mood of the people. The world may have been on the brink of war but Max Miller would keep the audience laughing. That night Miller wore a broad hat and a suit that looked more like a combination of colourful pyjamas.

The moment the orchestra played '*Mary from the Dairy*' and Max Miller made his appearance the audience seemed to light up like a chandelier. There were smiles and laughter all round. Frank and Honeysuckle grinned broadly. Spangler and Cherry broke out into happy smiles.

'Ere do you like the outfit lady!' Max Miller boomed to a giggling lady. 'Do you know what I am? I'm a travelling salesman and I'm ready for bed! Guess what I went for a walk in St. James's Park this afternoon and there were two old ladies feeding the ducks. Would you believe it, a naked man ran past? Honest lady! Naked as the day he was born with a few improvements thrown in! One of the old ladies had a stroke and the other one couldn't reach! The other day I was out walking the Sussex Downs near my home in Brighton and I was walking along this narrow cliff top path when a beautiful woman in a bright scarlet dress – yes, that's right lady, she was a scarlet woman – came walking towards me on this narrow path, not big enough for both of us. I wasn't sure whether to toss her off or to block her passage …!'

Max Miller's saucy near-the-knuckle repertoire went on for a long time with continuous laughter from the audience. Frank looked around him at the audience. Everyone was laughing and looked happy almost as if they had a premonition that the time was coming when the tears would fall.

★★★

The day of real dramatic change came on Sunday, 3rd September 1939. On the surface there was nothing extraordinary about that day. Frank and his son had gone walking in the morning and all seemed well with the world. People were going about their chores in the garden and around the house. Families were out walking. There was a man with a barrel organ and a monkey who added some light relief to the morning.

Frank looked very smart that day. He was dressed in a sports jacket with an open neck shirt and he had slicked his hair back nicely shined courtesy of his favourite olive oil and eau-de-cologne mixture. Michael was dressed in what might have been termed as 'Sunday best'. He wore it very reluctantly. Michael was always worried that some of the local kids might have seen him in it and laughed at him or called him a sissy. They didn't though, thank goodness.

It had been a pleasant morning and they were on their way home for dinner. When they were walking through their home suburb the streets were virtually deserted. Michael sensed that his father was struck by the quiet and desolation of the moment, the feeling of peace in the streets. It was definitely the calm before the storm clouds of war that would sweep across the world.

They walked along past a house where the door was open and the wireless was on rather loud. Frank stopped suddenly in his tracks as he recognised the voice on the airwaves. He rummaged in his pockets for change and handed Michael some coins.

'Here you are son. Go and get Mum a box of chocolates from that shop over there.' He pointed. 'Meet me back here.'

Michael went across to the shop unaware that his father was standing outside the terraced house listening to the wireless broadcast. From within the house the Prime Minister, Neville Chamberlain, told the nation that Britain was now at war with Germany. When Michael returned with the box of chocolates for his mother he found his father looking down at the floor with a feeling of sadness engulfing him. He looked at Frank and knew that all was not well.

'Are you alright Dad?' he asked meekly.

He turned to look at Michael. 'You're back already?' He was definitely downcast and he spoke quietly in the tone of a voice which betrayed shock. 'Got those chocolates for Mum?'

'Yeah,' said Michael raising the box in the air. 'Thought these would be nice.'

'They'll do nicely son. Come on let's go.' Frank and Michael started to walk back to Grenadier Guard Road and then he let out a sigh. 'Oh son, you'll never guess what?'

'What's the matter, Dad?'

'That house back there had the door open and the wireless was on. I hate to tell you this son. It was Chamberlain telling the country that we're now at war with Germany.'

'At war!' Michael exclaimed.

'I'm afraid so Mick,' Frank confirmed. 'I thought after that last lot in fourteen-eighteen that that would be it. It was frightful. But no – off we go again. We haven't learnt a thing!'

'What happens now?'

'Tomorrow the enlistment offices for the Army, Navy and Air Force will be full. There will be emergency services set up. New rules laid down. Yes everything will change.'

'You're not going to join up are you Dad?' Michael asked in all innocence.

This question brought a smile to Frank's face. 'Gosh, you're joking aren't you son? I did my bit in the trenches in the fourteen-eighteen show.

71

Got gassed for my efforts and my chest has never been the same since. Besides I'm a bit over the hill anyway. I'm in my forties you know. There might be a job at home I could do. Dunno what though. But I'll be doing my bit. Home Guard maybe. Air raid warden perhaps.'

'It might not last all that long. A few months maybe.'

'I wish I could be certain of that Mick. That's what we all thought when the last one started. I don't mean to sound discouraging but I've got to be honest with you. It could be a long haul. This one could be very different.'

The way Frank had spoken made his son feel anxious at that moment. The anxiety didn't last long. They crossed over the road and entered Grenadier Guard Road. Unexpectedly Frank broke out into a huge smile. At one house there was the always reliable Dolly Mandolino who carried out the same daily routine whether there was a tempest or a heatwave.

Every day without fail Dolly would be down on her knees scrubbing the front doorstep. Always she wore a handkerchief on her head with knots tied at both ends. Dolly was a strong, robust and large lady in her sixties who had lived in the East End all her life. She had a booming voice that was typical of her no-nonsense attitude.

Frank looked across at her with great affection. The world would fall apart but Dolly would not change her way of life for anyone. When Moseley had marched down her neck of the woods she had made sure she had got her tuppenny ha'pence worth. Dolly had blackened eyes and broken noses of several blackshirts with her fists in the grandiose punch up that followed.

'Look at that son!' Frank said admiringly. 'The British Bulldog spirit lives on!' He called out to her. 'Morning, Dolly! How are you sweetheart?'

Dolly boomed her reply. 'Top of the world, Frank! Mind you, I've got fluid on my lungs, my liver's packed up, the old rheumatism's causing me havoc, the arthritis is giving me hell to pay in me old legs, and my backside don't 'arf ache but apart from that, I'm top of the world and fighting fit! How's yourself?'

Frank wore a broad grin. 'Mustn't grumble as they say.' He tried to be serious. 'Did you hear Chamberlain's broadcast this morning? We're at war. Again!'

Dolly's reply was very eloquent. 'Yeah I heard it. Cobblers to the bleedin' lot of 'em! Cobblers to bleedin' 'itler! We'll kick their bleedin' arses if they come down here won't we Frank? 'Ere you ain't seen my bleedin' milkman 'ave ya? I'm dying for a cuppa and I ain't got no milk at 'ome!'

Frank turned to Michael and said, 'Son! With spirit like that England will never be defeated! Don't worry about Hitler and his mob invading the country. They'll never get past Bethnal Green!'

He was right. Dolly had every bit as much fight in her as the combined weight of the armed services.

By the time they got home Honeysuckle was laying the table for Sunday dinner. She was singing to herself as she moved around the room. They knew that she always listened to the wireless on a Sunday morning and would probably have heard Chamberlain's address to the nation so Michael was a little confused how his Mum could continue to be happy. If he had been a little older he would have known that very little fazed the people around their way. Dolly and Honeysuckle were typical of that breed who continue regardless because that was the nature of their characters.

'Hello Frank, hello Michael. Did you have a nice walk?' she asked.

'Yes love. Very nice walk. Dinner smells terrific.' Frank made no mention of the announcement of war. Surprisingly it was Honeysuckle who brought up the subject.

'It's just about ready for serving.' Her expression changed and with it the tone of her voice. 'Frank I heard on the wireless. Chamberlain said that... '

'I know,' Frank interjected. 'A house down the road had the door open. I could hear it in the street.'

Michael hovered around with the box of chocolates his father had sent him to buy earlier.

'Well that's it then I suppose. There's nothing we can do,' Honeysuckle said with an air of finality.

Frank sighed deeply. 'That puts paid to my ambitions for us all. A new start in Kent or Australia is going to be out,' he added hopefully, 'for a while anyway.'

'As I told you once before, we'll always come through. The three of us will always survive.'

'With your support Honeysuckle I can always battle on. We saw Dolly down the road cleaning her step. If the enemy come anywhere near old Dolly she'll take the lot on singlehanded and beat the dust out of them!'

'Sit yourselves down,' said Honeysuckle. She began to put the plates on the table. Michael reached for the box of chocolates.

'Dad,' said Michael, waving the box of chocolates in front of him.

'What is it son?'

'These Dad!' Michael said, handing him the box. 'You haven't given Mum the box of chocolates yet.'

Honeysuckle smiled warmly at Frank. In one splendid moment on a day when sombre news had dominated the airwaves they found that their affection for each other was everlasting.

★★★

Far away in New South Wales, Australia, a small group were gathered around the wireless at Endeavour Downs cattle station. Doris and Jack sat together. Roy Lane sat alongside his wife Josie and their son Terry. Johnny McCullough and Freddie Bannan poured themselves a beer and sipped it slowly. Then across the airwaves came the voice of the Australian Prime Minister Robert Menzies.

'Fellow Australians. It is my melancholy duty to inform you officially that in consequence of the persistence by Germany in her invasion of Poland, Great Britain has declared war upon her and that, as a result, Australia is also at war'.

For a moment they all sat quietly. Then almost on cue all eyes seemed to focus on Jack. He looked concerned. He knew of all of them he was still young enough to serve.

'Does this mean you'll be going Jack?' Doris asked, in a quiet voice. He put his arm around her and nodded slightly. What a way to start married life he thought, by having to go to war.

★★★

At home in Grenadier Guard Road a few days later Michael came in from school to find his father and mother sat at the table looking apprehensive. They smiled warmly at him but there was an obvious air of concern about them they could not disguise.

'Sit down Michael,' his mother said.

'What is it Mum? Have I done something wrong?' he asked.

Frank tousled his hair and said reassuringly, 'No mate. Not at all. The whole world is going to change for us. Dramatically I'm afraid. All over Britain kids are going to be evacuated. There's a war on and big cities are always the targets.'

'What your Dad is saying,' Honeysuckle tried to emphasise, 'is that children will be leaving their parents to go to the country. Devon. Somerset. Norfolk. To stay with relatives and carers.'

'And some overseas even,' Frank added. 'To places like Canada, the States…and places where they might have family…like…well Australia even.'

At once Michael knew what this meant. A tear formed in his eye. His Dad moved quickly to quell his fears.

'Your Aunt Doris and Uncle Jack … they'll be so pleased to see you. Hopefully it won't be long. Don't worry son. It'll be fine.'

★★★

So, along with many other children of those wartime years, Michael became an evacuee. Frank and Honeysuckle reluctantly but with good intentions sent him to Australia to join Jack and Doris in the Outback. The memories of that day of departure were very mixed and emotional. At the station parents hugged their children. How hard it was to say goodbye for so many and the tears were being shed all around. For Michael it had all happened so quickly. Just a short time ago he had been a pupil at Britannia Street School going home to his Mum and Dad at Grenadier Guard Road. Now his whole world had changed.

In years to come Michael would remember his father at the station in his cap and overcoat giving him last minute advice, a reassuring hug, exuding love and trying to be cheerful. Somehow his face of sadness and a shaky voice of cheer told a different story. If Michael had known then that he would never see his Dad again he would have hugged him; told him how grateful he was for everything he had done. If only he could have perceived what the future would hold. How could he had ever known? And his dear lovely Mum putting on her bravest face, always as firm as the Rock of Gibraltar, as loving as ever a woman could be of her family. Reluctantly he boarded the train with the other children.

In a moment of panic Michael pushed open the window and reached out to his parents. They gripped each other's hands tightly for the last time. The train engines started up. They released their grip. Then in a matter of minutes the train was rolling out of the station towards the docks with the smoke streaming across the window. Out of the corner of his eye Michael could just catch a final glimpse of his parents together. None of them could possibly have envisaged just what the future would hold.

Ten

The sea voyage to Australia seemed to take forever. The reason for this was because the normal route through the Suez Canal was curtailed due to the war. Normal shipping lanes were avoided. Michael learned later that they sailed the longest possible way around and often miles out of their way for fear of encounter with enemy ships.

When the boat finally arrived at Pyrmont Docks in Sydney, all the youngsters on board were caught up in a flurry of mixed emotions. Michael looked out from the side of the boat and there, amid the crowd on the wharf, were Jack and Doris waving to him. Their faces seemed to reflect the atmosphere of this country. They were sunny and golden, warm and welcoming.

After that arduous trip down under by sea there followed a long railway journey through the bush. Michael's new life began in a country that had more wide open spaces and infinite blue skies than he could ever have imagined from his youthful home in Grenadier Guard Road. And sunshine! He had never seen such blazing sunshine that soaked every sight and scene in golden light bringing it to its ultimate splendour. Looking out of the truck as Freddie Bannan drove them from the railway to Endeavour Downs station the sights and sounds of the bush stunned him. His feelings of longing for home were suddenly overtaken by the excitement of the new things that lay before him.

Michael would always remember with a heart-stopping thrill his first views of such openness of land, of hot dry harsh brown plains, ghost-like trees that spreadeagled in sunlight-enhanced colours; silver-white gleaming against a Pacific blue sky a crinkled mahogany skyrocketing and withering in the glaring sun. He had never seen such a variety of unusual looking trees like the stringy bark jacaranda, gum and baobab. It would take some time before he would realise that this land with its brashness of character and contour line and merciless weather conditions yielded a sensitivity and spirit of unparalleled uniqueness.

The day after he arrived at Endeavour Downs station several of them went on horseback for Michael's introduction to the bush. The sudden change in his lifestyle was something that he could never have imagined happening to him. He could not grasp all the dramatic changes that had been inflicted on him with the advent of war.

To be here in this strange sweltering land was a miracle to him. Just a short time before Michael had lived with the expectation that, like his father before him, he would work in a factory and the East End would forever be his home.

Now in this place where it was 120 degrees in the shade, coloured tropical birds flew high above him. In the distance big red kangaroos hopped shyly into obscurity. He nervously rode a horse across harsh land similar to where he had walked through industrial estates to Britannia Street School. It was the sound of the bush that fascinated him. This is something one has to experience to understand. Cicadas in the trees made noises like volts of electricity surging through power cables. Tropical birds squawked so differently from the cries of the English starling and the robins that landed on the window boxes in Grenadier Guard Road. Far beyond, the noise of distant cattle herds echoed across the horizon. Then there would be the sound of total silence on an open plain with only a huge red sun burning against the fierce orange desert.

Not all of the land was bare and barren that their horses gently jogged across. There were occasional clumps of trees and bushes interspersed at infrequent intervals with only sparse vegetation. Roy Lane, Johnny McCullough rode with Jack, Doris and Michael. It was an eye-opener for Michael to be in a part of the world where big, bronzed, wrinkled men rode these plains. He had often heard people who didn't know the men of the bush describe Australians as suntanned Cockneys. In some ways that was way off the mark. Both races of people had their own jargon, their slang and phrases unique only to them. Yet he did feel at ease with them. He sensed no similarity between the Australian and the Cockney but from his first day at Endeavour Downs station he felt as if he was among his own people. In truth it was possibly their directness of manner; their sometimes blatant harsh honesty and tendency to look at everything square on in a way of fair interpretation.

Roy Lane was a genuine man. He had all the strengths that came to the fore in times of crisis. He led by example and initiative. Roy was also eloquent in his way of speaking. On that day Michael heard Roy, Jack and Johnny indulging in conversation and each man spoke with surprising authority and knowledge. Johnny McCullough, whom he had thought on first meeting to be a roughneck Scotsman, turned out to be a soulful character who spoke at times in an almost poetical and lyrical fashion.

'I'd like to show you a lot more of Endeavour Downs,' said Roy, 'but to tell you the truth, the whole place is probably the size of six or seven English counties!'

'That big?!' Michael was genuinely surprised.

'Absolutely son,' Roy replied with a smile. He always knew the size of the station bewildered people. 'It quite surprised your aunt there. Isn't that right Doris?'

Doris smiled. She had happily taken to her new life with a zest that quite surprised her. With a wide brimmed hat and a countrywoman's droving outfit she managed to retain her femininity despite her drastic change of fashion to suit her new environment.

'Jack told me what I was coming out to,' Doris replied. 'You're right though. The size and space really threw me. It was beyond my imagination.'

Jack weighed in with his explanation. 'A lot of people from the coastal cities get a shock too. They come up from Melbourne and Sydney expecting to see a few plots of land with some woollies running loose and a couple of beef cattle in a back yard. Then they see acres and acres of land still to be cultivated. The kind of land which is either too dry under the sun or if we have a big wet then it's ravaged by flood waters. It's something people never really get the grasp of until they've lived here for a while and then they either love it or loath it.' He turned around to Johnny. 'Would that be right, mate?'

From beneath his bushman's hat Johnny looked up and smiled. 'An acquired taste you might say. I've been to many places in my time as a seaman. There's something about the bush that has a flavour and allure about it that has seduced many a man from many a nation.'

'You add a bit of colour to the place,' Roy added. 'We meet all kinds out here. Good. Bad. Indifferent. Get a few runaways too from the city. Blokes running out on debts, wives, police charges. We try not to ask unless the sergeant has told us to watch out for a couple of crook characters.

Sometimes a swaggie will drop by who'll ask to do a few days of work without pay, just for a few decent meals and a good night's sleep. Makes life interesting I guess. I can imagine how young Michael there must be viewing this place.' He winked at the lad who was listening intently to him. 'A lot different from factories and terraces in the English provinces. I'm an avid reader myself in some of the more quieter moments of life here and I read how England spawned the Industrial Revolution from which the great tradesmen learned skills and craftsmanship with their tools that they took to the far corners of the globe. When they landed here they must have seen plenty they could get their teeth into. A great big land mass with only the Aboriginals to begin with. A place for settlements to be established and populated and new cities to be built. Towns to flourish. Land to be tilled, fertilised and watered. Crops to be grown. Cattle to breed and market. Water resources to plan. Artesian wells to construct. Power supplies and energy to organise, railways and roads to build.'

'That was only the half of it.' Jack was never slow in giving his opinion. 'Not only did they have a land to develop. More importantly, they had a history to start. And for such a young nation didn't we show the rest of the world what we could do? By golly Roy, we've come a long way in 150 years, haven't we?' There was a real enthusiasm in the way Jack spoke. 'From a nation of convict foundations to a place that offers promise for everyone who wants to give it a real go. Yes mate, we've got a lot to be proud of. It's not just the Anzac tradition. It's the whole makeup of our country; the pioneers; the explorers; the Gold Rush days; the Kelly Gang; explorers like Wentworth, Blaxland, Burke and Wills. How we came through the Depression years.'

At this point Roy led the small group of horse riders up onto a high ridge. They dismounted from their horses and took in the remarkable view of the land that lay before them. Michael walked to one side away from the others and looked out at it in awe. It was probably then he realised just how much space surrounded him. Years of living in London in an area of terraced houses and factories made him realise just how small and confined his world had been. Standing there in the Outback Michael felt incredibly free and calm within. He suddenly thought how much his father would have given to have been able to enjoy the experience of being in this place. He felt excited and thrilled, eager and interested in what the future would hold. Before he had always accepted the life he had. Never ever again would he just accept things the way they were. He would always strive to improve.

Michael walked back to where his Aunt Doris stood talking with Roy, Johnny and Jack. Roy seemed more like a western cowboy than an Outback jackaroo. He pushed his hat back and smiled.

'Look at all that,' he said to Doris. 'I've been here years ya' know. Still find it hard to believe that's all Endeavour Downs' land. All of that down there is up to me to look after. It's a hell of a big job. Twenty or so years ago I started all that up. Who would ever have believed that?'

Doris appeared sympathetic. 'Roy I know the numbers are down on the farm what with the war but if there's anything I can do I'll pitch in as best as I can.'

'What do you want me to do Mr Lane?' Michael asked.

Roy smiled broadly. 'For a start you can call me Roy. Mister is a term of address for the city. There's a fair bit of work you can do if you want. No pressure, son. But any help you can give us would be more than welcome. You could help out in the shearing shed as one of the tar boys. Johnny does a lot of carpentry work around the place. He needs some help. You could go with Freddie one day. He rides the boundaries a lot fixing fences, bringing back any of our cattle that have wandered into the station next door.'

'I'll have a go,' Michael volunteered.

The small group returned to the station later that day. Michael knew that this was a chapter of his life he was going to enjoy.

Eleven

In 1940 Frank and Honeysuckle Forbes lived through the terrible time of the Blitz. Bombs rained fiercely down on the city of London with the East End taking the worst of it. The night sky was ignited with lights and sparks, and fires and smoke. Casualty lists grew. Ambulance and fire services were permanently busy. For Londoners the full terror of the war was brought to their front doorsteps and many homes and lives were lost. But for Frank who had bitterly regretted the wasted years of working long hours for little reward in a rundown factory, these terrible times had perhaps helped him to find one of the most important roles in his life.

With the advent of the war Frank had become an air-raid warden. His years of frustration with his everyday humdrum life had been circumvented by fate. Purpose had been restored to him. Knowing that he had a very important job to do he had become one of the courageous team of men who protected the civilian population from attack. He tackled his new role with enthusiasm.

During one of the heaviest raids of the Blitz, Frank was on duty at a London underground tube station where the courage he had always possessed came to the fore. The raids that night had been terrifying. When the sound of the air raid sirens had been heard the people on the streets were shown to safety. It was obvious that the bombing was going to go on for a long time and many people had bedded down for the night. There were long hours ahead to endure.

It was not only the civilian men and women there but children and many personnel from the services. One extraordinary sight was of a well-to-do couple there swilling back champagne. The lady wore furs and jewellery and her companion, a dinner suit and bow tie. Frank passed by the two as he led some women and children to safety.

'Would you like a glass of champagne?' the lady jokingly asked.

'I'll have one when the war's over, love,' Frank replied dryly and he moved along the platform. The underground station was beginning to look pretty well full that night. Even down below the outside noise was penetrating the walls.

Frank made his way back up to the exit. Outside people were running from all directions. Beams were soaring upwardly but the enemy aircraft were dropping bombs with ferocity on many buildings and streets nearby.

'This way please!' he called out anxiously to the people on the streets. They quickly responded. A bomb exploded barely a hundred yards away. 'Over here for heaven's sake!' Frank called to more people.

In his anxiety he ran over and helped some of the older ones to safety. He carried children down and handed them to the other air-raid wardens. Then he returned to the exit again. He had antagonised his chest badly that night from all of his running around and several times he had to stop to catch his breath.

Suddenly a bomb struck a residential building close to the station. Glass, wood and bricks hurtled through the air. Flames surged up towards the sky. There were shouts and cries and screams punctuating the air. The sheer terror of it filtered through to Frank who froze his eyes in horror at the spectacle. Straightaway he made a dash from the exit of the underground railway and moved into the decimated building. It was a terrible sight that befell him and he pushed his way through the rubble and the wood. With every ounce of strength he could muster, he pulled out the survivors and the injured. Frank's face was covered in dirt and smoke, pieces of the building rained down on him as its foundations fell apart all around.

The fire and ambulance crews arrived while Frank carried the survivors out. He went back inside one more time. He fought his way through to a corner where there were two children cowering with fright. There were bricks and timbers in the way and Frank pushed his way clear. The children's parents were lying dead on the floor. For one ghastly moment he was shocked by what he had seen. Never in this life had he had to deal with anything like this before. His eyes clouded over with tears.

'Come on sweetheart. Come on sonny Jim, let's get you out of here.' Frank was shaking in sadness as he reached down for the children. He tried to be as soft and sensitive as he could be in such terrible circumstances.

At that crucial moment a fire flared up close by. He could not waste a single precious moment. Without hesitation he grabbed each of the children by the hand and rushed them out. A man from the ambulance helped him and took the young children aside. The building they had been in soared with flames and started to collapse. He looked on in shock for the building had inadvertently become a funeral pyre for the parents of the two children. His eyes flooded with tears.

Frank was about to move away when he was struck by one of his coughing bouts. He grabbed his handkerchief and dabbed his mouth. To his horror there were spots of blood. He was shocked at the realisation that his chest complaint had been stirred and the condition antagonised by the events of the night. Frank realised he could do no more and went back to the shelter. One of the ambulancemen approached him.

'We'll get someone to have a look at you,' he said.

The courage of the moment for Frank was dampened by the fact that he realised he was in real trouble healthwise. 'I'm alright,' he croaked in the hoarsest of voices and lying to himself at the same time. 'I'm more worried about those kiddies.'

'They'll be alright,' the man said. 'The lad's in the ambulance – they'll take care of them now.' He looked at Frank. He could see how sick he was. 'Come on mate. Let's get you down anyway and we'll swab you down. You've got a face like a coalminer.'

Frank reluctantly went down below. He wanted to do more for the people who had been injured but he knew it was beyond him to help. His job was in the air-raid shelter. He gazed down at his clothes. They were stained blood red from his fit of coughing. Dark, red blood. Frank shuddered. Surely at only forty-eight years of age this wasn't happening. Not yet please God, he thought. He wanted to see Michael grow up. His face reflected the horror of what was happening. Then as he descended into the underground station his mind concentrated on the here and now. People were bedding down for the night.

The noise of the Blitz continued all through the night. In the air-raid shelter the people seemed to be registering every conceivable emotion on their faces. During the night the air-raid wardens did their best to placate the people and keep some sort of morale together.

Eventually exhaustion took over and even though Frank had fought hard to keep up his strength, he succumbed to sheer tiredness and passed out on the platform. He woke up intermittently and did his duties as an air-raid warden but he felt ill and tired, and had to keep lying down.

It was a terrifying sight that greeted Frank when he finally made his way home through the East End. He stood aghast at the bomb damage visible everywhere. He would run, then walk and stop; noting how some houses and factories had taken a direct hit. He walked slowly along Grenadier Guard Road and breathed a sigh of relief when he saw that the street was virtually intact although nearby areas had been damaged.

In those other streets there were helpers and first-aid workers attending to adults and children alike. He stopped to survey the scene. With absolute dismay he removed his helmet and ran his hands through his hair. The combination of exhaustion and emotion within brought him close to breaking point. He stood there wiping his eyes and trembling. It was a while before he could get a grip on himself and carry on.

Across the road Dolly was at her step scrubbing it as usual. She was resilient and stubborn at all times. Frank gazed on in awe, admiration and amazement. He knew that folk in the East End were a hardy lot and very little fazed them.

Dolly was aware of his presence as Frank crossed the road.

'I've been doing this front step for thirty-five years. I ain't going to let anything stop me now. All night long I listened to the Luftwaffe bombing the blazes out of us and I thought to myself I'm going to carry on tomorrow in spite of them!' Then with a blooming flourish she added, 'If bleedin' 'itler comes down this street I'm going to give him a piece of my mind!'

Dolly stood up and looked directly at Frank. Her eyes were red with tears. The two of them flung their arms around each other.

'I'm a tough old basket Frank. Some folk round here have got nothing after last night,' she added in sadness, 'that includes your mate Spangler and Cherry.'

At once Frank thought that the absolute worst had happened.

'What? Spangler and Cherry? Are they …?'

'They're alright Frank. They got out of their house just minutes before … They are with Honeysuckle. You haven't got a place to work at though. The factory took a direct hit.'

'Oh my God,' Frank gasped. 'Any casualties?'

'Just one. Charlie Atkins the night watchman,' she replied. 'You haven't seen the other places round here. Factories, street, trolley buses, trams. It was a very bad night.'

Frank looked downcast. 'All those people. How terrible.' He paused. 'Come down and join us for a meal Dolly when you're ready.'

'I will. Go home and see Honeysuckle.' The tough old bird that Dolly was finally broke her composure. A tear trickled from her eyes. 'Its been a long night.'

Frank rubbed her arm and walked down the street. Honeysuckle had been waiting nervously for him. When she saw him she sighed with relief. Honeysuckle ran from the house to greet him. They embraced in the middle of Grenadier Guard Road.

Later they all sat around the table in a somewhat sombre mood. Dolly had come down to join them. Spangler and Cherry had settled in unaware that by the fate and circumstances of war this would be their home for the duration. Such was the spirit of the time that many of the people in the East End opened their homes to strangers and friends and just about any victim of the Blitz who lost their place of abode.

After a subdued silence Spangler finally broke the ice of the atmosphere. 'Oh it was a fearful night, Frank.' It was not the normally jovial Spangler who spoke although there was a latent spark of humour just waiting to be aroused in his eyes.

'I'm really, really sorry about your house Spangler,' Frank said trying to be as sympathetic as he could be in the circumstances.

'We only had a couple of rooms there,' said Cherry wistfully. 'It wasn't really our house, but it was our home for nigh on twenty years. All those years. All those blessed memories. They all vanished in a night.'

'Cherry and I had so many happy times there,' Spangler said quietly. 'And now its been taken from us. There was something in me telling Cherry to run out, while we had the chance. Oh bejeezers! Five minutes later and...'

'Don't think about it Spangler,' Honeysuckle cut in quickly. 'You can stay with us for as long as you need.'

Frank added his verbal postscript. 'You won't hear any argument from me against that either. That goes for you Dolly. We'll look after you.'

'I can sit here and be bull-headed about how I won't let the Hun kick me out of the house I shared with my Arthur.' Dolly answered asserting her independence as always, 'But common sense tells me if I want to live to fight another day I might go and stay with my sister in Devon for a while.'

'We'll miss you when you go Dolly,' Cherry added.

Spangler turned to Frank and spoke in a hushed voice. 'You know one of your fellow air-raid wardens dropped round early today. He said you were really full of guts last night, going into burning homes and carrying people out.'

Honeysuckle looked on beaming with pride at the hidden courage her husband had. Dear Frank, she thought, a battler all his life. Looking far, far older than his forty-eight years, always a worrier about his family that he loved so much, yet whom he felt he had failed so badly. Right at that moment Honeysuckle could not have felt prouder. His courage and compassion had shown themselves at a time to quote Winston Churchill, 'cometh the hour'.

Spangler's words did not have a good effect on Frank. Rather more than anything it jolted Frank into talking about the previous night. He was tired and weary. His eyes were red with tiredness and he tried to force a smile but the emotional upset he had experienced together with his own health problems had steadily broken his resistance down to traumatic events.

'I – I wish I could have been here.' He put his hands to his face as if he was trying to drain away the expression he wore. 'I was so worried when the bombs started dropping.' Everyone was listening attentively. Frank's words seemed to cut the air. There were looks of concern about his state of mind on both Spangler and Dolly's faces. 'I saw this block of apartments go up in a blaze when it took a hit. There were two children …' His eyes flooded with tears. When he spoke it was with a sob evident in his faltering voice. 'Two little kiddies. A girl and boy not more than four and five I guess. They were frightened out of their lives. They were in a corner and their Mum and Dad were … were gone. It's no good seeing a couple of kids orphaned like that. Then the fire started and the flames went up all around. So I grabbed the kids and we ran through. An ambulance fellow looked after them. I spent the night in the air-raid shelter. It's the look on the kiddies' faces that I'm never going to forget till the end of my days.'

Honeysuckle had never seen her husband so emotional. It upset her deeply. She wanted to say something but could not find the words and she found herself sitting in a solitude of silence. Luckily Spangler broke in. He had the knack of always being able to find words even at the most awkward of times.

'We've seen all this before Frank. We were in the trenches together and we were young fellows in the thick of it all. Young lads of sixteen or seventeen died. I've not forgotten either. This is the consequence of war. There's no glamour in it! It's about death, destruction, heartbreak and the loss of loved ones that once sat round the table and will never do again. It's about the loss of a brother or a dad on some foreign battlefield. It's about the kids who lose their mummy and daddy in a bomb attack before they've even got to know them. And more than anything it's about the young men who die before they make their mark on the world as a decent human being, a friend or potential husband, who never knew a trade and never wasted a few bob on a Saturday night chasing the wrong kind of girl!'

'We'll be seeing a darn sight more though won't we?' Cherry said firmly without raising her voice. 'We've got to be strong. Nothing's going to shake us.'

The real voice of the East End spoke up with resounding effect. 'Gawd!' Dolly always spoke as she found. 'We're a sombre lot today. Come on all you good folk! Let's snap out of it. I've got no time for dwelling on what's happened. Life's not for maudlin. It's for fighting on no matter what. We're not a country to be kicked about are we?'

'Of course not!' Honeysuckle responded. 'I'm just glad our Mick is far away from it all.'

From a bottle on the table Dolly poured each one a glass. 'Well here's to the lads and lasses of our armed forces and old Winnie, gawd help the old bulldog, and to those we've loved and lost.'

'I'd like to second that … and here's to the folk around here. May God bless them all,' said Spangler.

They all raised their glasses.

Twelve

Michael rolled over in his bunk bed. It was far too hot to sleep. He looked across to the clock and he was surprised to see it was only four o'clock in the morning. Already there were noises indicating the work at Endeavour Downs station was beginning. The sound of doors opening and closing. A horse whinnied. Drovers chatting amiably. Cattle getting restless. The general stirring of a great cattle station coming to life. The sound of voices carried and Michael heard the words, 'Jack's leaving today'. Indeed he was. Only recently had Jack completed his Army training and he was home from leave for a while. Today he had to return to Puckapanyal in Victoria before being sent to Darwin in the Northern Territory.

Outside, the darkness had lifted and the changing shades of the sky intermingled with the golden brown of the bush created a range of pastoral colours across which jackaroos rode. Michael looked out of the window in fascination at the sight. For a moment he thought of his parents far away in Blitz-besieged London. He and his Aunt Doris had listened to the news they received and prayed that all was well with Frank and Honeysuckle.

In the year or so Michael had been there he entered his new life with all the energy he could muster. He had felt determined to do his very best at all times. While the war raged on in Europe he had led an interesting life. The first job he had worked on was in the shearing shed. With Roy's son, Terry, he had become a tar boy. Michael was fascinated by the routine that the shearers carried out day after day without complaint. The scene of these strong men in competition with each other was a clash of the titans. It was combat and skill to view.

Inside the shearing shed a line of muscular men in tank top vests stood at the ready. The starting bell rang and the shearers pulled some thickly wooled sheep out and began the process. It was hard gruelling work. But for Michael to watch it was an Olympic spectacle. It was back-breaking work which was particularly tough on the taller shearers. They had to crouch their backs as they moved the clippers across the sheep's fleeces. The wool fell off into huge bundles on the floor. Terry and Michael quickly swept it away and put the wool into bags. They were the tar boys and their job could be loosely classified as sweeping, bundling and bagging. The gun shearer was particularly energetic. He just never stopped and when the day was over he walked away wringing wet in perspiration. Some of the others were in a state of near collapse.

When Michael walked into the dining room at Endeavour Downs he was surprised to see Jack standing there proudly in his Army uniform. Roy and Freddie were with him and Doris stood by them.

'Are you going to wish me luck young Michael?' he asked stretching his hand out to him. Michael took it. Jack had a strong grip.

'We always seem to be saying goodbye,' said Michael in his youthful way, not realising how accurate his words were. 'Someone's always leaving.'

Jack smiled at him and put his arm around Doris. 'Are you ready boys?'

'Let's go then,' said Freddie and the small group went outside to the small lorry that would take them to Endeavour Downs station. Michael waved to his Uncle Jack unaware that he would never see him again. Jack had been a warm and amiable uncle to Michael. The pity of it all was that they had only spent a brief time together although this dinky-die figure had made an enormous impression on the boy.

Often when he wasn't working as a tar boy Michael helped out with the cattle branding. He admired the skill of the men who endeavoured to pull the huge beasts down and brand them. He sat on the fence the first time next to an Aboriginal stockman and Johnny McCullough. Both men had no hesitation about jumping into the corral and tackling the fierce animals. Eventually Michael learned to tackle this job but faced with one of those huge beasts it was definitely courage acquired.

By far and away the job he enjoyed the most was riding the boundaries. He accompanied Freddie Bannan on these rides which meant being out in the bush for weeks at a time. This was a job for someone who loved solitude and had an independent self-sufficient streak about themselves. Undoubtedly this job suited Freddie perfectly. He loved the open country and the peace of being his own man. Freddie was at his happiest. He would brew up tea in a billy and make the tastiest damper bread using flour and water, or as a substitute if he had a bottle of beer with him he would use that as part of the liquid ingredients. Michael didn't ask what he made the damper from. He would just watch him make it and enjoy the taste.

From a distance the figures of Freddie and Michael on horseback would have been like minute silhouettes against the vast expanse of bush landscape. There were billabongs which they always camped by and where more often or not Freddie would spin out his own thoughts on life to Michael. Freddie was glad of the company. He was plain speaking. Michael admired his thoughts on life. For some reason he wished that his father Frank could have met him. He thought they would have got on well.

They camped at a clump of trees by one of those billabongs on one more memorable occasion than the others. Perhaps it was because of the things that followed on. Michael was not sure why but this particular ride was more easily remembered.

The night began to fall. The sun lowered very quickly as the night shadows fell. In the background there were noises of insects and squawking birds.

Freddie removed his hat and ran his hand across his brow. 'By gosh, its been a warm one today hasn't it young Michael?'

'It seems to get hotter and hotter,' Michael agreed. By the billabong it was much cooler. 'I guess you are used to it?'

'You would think so. It doesn't cool much at night either. We're camping here tonight. To coin a phrase 'under the shade of a coolibah tree'. There's water to drink there, to swim and wash in, and let the horses rest by. It'll be a bit cooler here tonight. Well maybe one degree cooler perhaps.'

They camped by the billabong waters that night. The glow of the burning red campfire flickered in the luminous reflection enhanced by the huge moon in the night sky. Freddie was a good bush cook. His damper bread and stew followed by a mug of billy-boiled tea was as good as any hotel meal to Michael. He was a friendly man. In Michael's initial shyness he wondered how to talk to this man who was over three times his age. He finally found the question that was the trigger to him entering into conversation.

'Why did you leave the city to come out to – to this … ?'

Freddie thought about this for a moment. 'Good question indeed young man. And I can quite understand why you ask.'

'My Uncle Jack said you used to be a bank clerk in Adelaide,' remarked Michael.

Freddie explained. 'Some difference between that job and this one I'll grant you. So why did I leave the city for the bush? Well I was a young fellow with a lot of high spirits I guess. Too high spirited to work in a place like a bank where I was keeping tabs on people's accounts; how much they needed to borrow to buy a house or a car or some new clothes for a relative's wedding. Mind you, I'm not knocking working in a bank. It's a good job for those interested in security and who enjoy city life and going home to their place in the suburbs. But not for me though. I'm interested in living life to the utmost. And I suppose if I think about it I'm like a lot of blokes who come out to the bush from the city – and from abroad I might add – the stage isn't big enough for us. We need the Outback because we sleep and breathe more easily. Does that make sense?'

Michael considered what he had heard. One thing puzzled him however. This was Freddie's addiction to a life of solitude. 'I think so. But don't you miss people?'

'People!' he exclaimed as though they were something who came from another planet. 'I miss some people. A few childhood mates. Some of my relatives. Most of them long gone. But by people I don't miss the crowds, queues at the picture house. I don't miss the difficulties of trying to get served in a restaurant or the chaos of people piling on to a tram or a bus. Perhaps more than anything I don't miss people's attitudes; you know the sort of thing I mean. The bloke and the Sheila who reckon they're always right and that the rest of the world is wrong. Neither do I miss the selfish person who believes the world should revolve around their every whim and wish. No son, I don't miss those city things. 'Yet in a way I love the people I know in the bush. They are a real special breed you know. Their friendship and loyalty has got a value worth more than the price of gold.'

'There aren't too many people though are there?' Michael pointed out.

'You're right there,' Freddie replied and then he added further to his explanation. 'But there's a mateship about people here. There has to be because the bush is so big. It can be so tough. I don't know too much about your part of the world in London other than a few weeks' leave I had there after I'd been fighting in Gallipoli and France in the last war. Do you know something though Mick? I reckon that the Aussie and maybe the true blue Cockney born within the sound of Bow Bells might be a lot more similar than we care to admit.'

'How do you make that out?' Michael was genuinely surprised that Freddie knew about Cockneys and Bow Bells.

'There's hardship in your part of the world. Right? Different kind though. People are broke. Struggle along. Maybe places they have to live in are pretty rough. We all heard about the Blitz in London over here. Your people are cheerful though. Got a good sense of humour about them. They take the rough with the smooth. Got a lot of courage without bluster. That's how the folk in the bush are. Their circumstances are different of course. Out here we face the ravages of the climate. Drought. Bushfire. Flood. We live through it all yet we get on with it because we have to. That's what life is all about isn't it? You take a fall. It hurts and it hurts. But you can't stay down. It's a lot better when you get up and have another go. The bush people pull together. If a bloke's got a problem a lot of people he doesn't even know will come out and give him a hand then just as quickly go off and head back to their place without asking for thanks. God bless 'em all. I've got so much time for them you wouldn't believe it.'

'Don't you ever wish you'd got married though?' Michael asked.

In the flash of an instant Freddie's eyes seemed to change to sadness. 'Oh I was married … once…when I was young.' He noticed the change in Michael's expression. 'That surprised you didn't it? Yeah, back before the First World War. Prettiest girl in Adelaide I reckon. We weren't married long.' His face took on a deeply sad expression. 'She died in childbirth. Lost the kid too.' He paused for reflection. 'Ah well … then came the war and off I went. Yeah, they were hard times for me.'

'Sounds like you had a hard life,' Michael said softly well aware that his own father Frank had known much suffering in his time too. 'The people here in the bush seem hard to me.'

'They are hard, son. Hard on the surface that is. A lot of them went through the Depression like your people in England and America did but they came through. What you don't see is the warmth and the generosity beneath the hard surface. You're only a youngster. You've got a lot to learn about people. Don't be quick to judge by what you see on the surface. I've met some city people who at first impression were the biggest pain in the – you could meet. When I got to know them – different story. Don't judge a book by its cover.'

'Some of the people I know back home are like that I suppose,' he said remembering some people who were grumpy looking but cheery natured.

'Battling spirits,' Freddie stated emphatically. 'That's what they'd be.' He relit his cigarette. 'Going back to what I was saying earlier about the pattern of life,' he added, 'and the similarities between people battling all over the world really. You know son, I don't reckon anyone has a life that's as smooth as silk. If they did it'd be pretty boring anyway wouldn't it? No my young friend, life in geographical terms is like an uncharted journey, full of peaks and sometimes valleys of despair and every now and again maybe a beautiful lush smooth plateau of comfort.'

'I like the way you speak,' Michael said admiringly. 'Johnny speaks in a similar manner. But your words are like those from a book.'

This remark in turn triggered another response from Freddie. 'Believe it or not Johnny, myself and Roy – well we're all blokes that like to read deeply. Roy's favourite subject is history. He's got a great sense of occasion has our Roy. He likes to read about agriculture and industry; how things have changed over the years. He's interested in the history of different types of farming going as far back as the days of the old English crofters. Now Johnny, there's a fellow who's packed a hell of a lot into his life. He's been everywhere. Johnny's got a lot of memories. He'll read about everything.'

'It surprises me. I would have thought people in the bush didn't have too much interest in books.' It was a naïve comment from Michael.

Freddie grinned at him. 'You're joking aren't you? If it wasn't for the shortwave or a good book, life would be pretty empty for many bush folk. Out here a lot of fellows spend a lot of time on their own. Out on the trail solitude is part of the way of life. I treat it as thinking time. It may surprise you that there's many a self-educated man in these parts. I know of couple of blokes who always carry a book of poetry in their saddlebags. I've stood out in the bush on my own and I've read out aloud. I have spoken out to the stars. Not a flaming soul in sight. Not a 'roo or a possum or a slithery old goanna around. Not even a stray swaggie with a blanket roll. I've stood right out there on my own and I've read from Richard 111. I've spoken Shakespeare, echoed Byron and Shelley and Rudyard Kipling's poem 'If' across the ranges and the plains with only the moon and the stars as my audience.'

'I don't make you out at all. You like poetry?' Michael was baffled by Freddie. In many ways he seemed to be a man of simple tastes and direct manner but it seemed as if he could talk knowledgeably on almost anything.

'Well,' he said, trying to explain his personality, 'It's the romance in my soul. I'm a kid at heart. Never quite grew up I guess. I'm still finding it hard at my age to separate the fantasy from the reality. Part of me yearns to be an Errol Flynn swashbuckler. Another part of me loves to read deeply, speak poetry and to try and act gentle. I'm not sure who I am at times. I like a few beers with the boys. I can laugh at a coarse joke. Don't tell them, mind! Then on the other hand I can go weak at the knees at the sight of a pretty woman and get tongue-tied and go all gawky. When I was younger I used to image a man's prestige in life could be measured by his successes. Now I know the truth of it is that a man is made great by his ability to handle his failures and circumstances.'

After a pause Michael said, 'I enjoyed listening to you talk.'

'Did you son?' he asked with a smile. 'I think I talk a bit too much myself.' He rolled over on his side. 'Time for sleep. We've got a long day tomorrow.'

It wasn't a great deal cooler during the night. Somehow Michael managed to sleep. He awoke at four o'clock as the sun began to rise. After a few of these rides along the boundaries he was still trying to get used to this pattern of life. For Freddie it was second nature to him. He slept like a log. He was a peaceful sleeper who only stirred slightly despite the heat which was surprisingly heavy even at this early stage of the day.

Michael lay on his back gazing at the incredibly clear sky. All around him the bush was coming to life. Above them the tropical birds of the bush flew across the sky and in and out of tree branches. The sound of insects buzzing started to get louder almost in harmony with the degrees of temperature as it got warmer. He sat up and rubbed his eyes. He was perspiring already. The billabong waters looked inviting. Michael was just contemplating whether or not to take a dip when he saw what he perceived to be a figure flashing through the trees.

Michael gazed on mystified for he was sure that he had seen something. Freddie was still sleeping soundly. The horses were grazing. Again Michael looked at the billabong. The sun's powerful beams were rendering the waters crystal clear. Already it was very warm. He could no longer resist the temptation. He walked towards the water and looked around apprehensively. Not for one minute did he imagine there would be anyone to see him swim naked in the billabong. But for one who had only ever gone swimming at Lambeth public baths, Michael abandoned all inhibitions. He shed his clothes and stepped into the refreshing water. It was blissful. Cleopatra could have her Egyptian baths of asses' milk. To Michael the coolness of this water was pure luxury.

He swam about enjoying the moment. Up above the sun's rays filtered through the trees in streamlined beams. For a moment he lay back in the water luxuriating in the coolness of it all. On one of the trees a kookaburra or 'laughing jackass' appeared followed by several others who positioned themselves on the branches. Michael stared at it in fascination. Suddenly the birds erupted into a sound that resembled raucous laughter. For moments it seemed to him as if the birds were in their own way laughing uproariously at his state of nakedness. It brought a smile to Michael's face and he found himself laughing. In another instant the laughter became amplified. It was the sound of children laughing followed by adults. He was terrified and sprang up from the water.

To his dismay and shock he realised that he was surrounded. There were figures in the trees and around the billabong. Michael was aghast in horror. For all around were roaming Aborigines laughing and speaking in their dialect; the words of which were totally incomprehensible to him. Then some of the children started entering the water and playfully splashed him. He realised with relief that they were good natured and friendly. They swam up and down together and threw water over each other. The little Aborigine boys had broad smiles lighting up their chocolatey-brown faces. For a while they played and then Michael decided it was time to leave the water.

Quickly he grabbed his clothes but the Aborigines beckoned him to follow them. They pointed to a few ramshackle dwellings in the distance a short way from the billabong. He was hesitant to follow. He wanted to return to where Freddie was still sleeping. Michael could not understand a single word these people were saying to him. All he could see was this mass of brown faces chatting away. In the end it was curiosity that caused him to go with them.

At the Aboriginal camp Michael looked around in absolute amazement. In his youthful ignorance he had known nothing of the way these people lived. Not even in his classes at Britannia Street School had he ever learned anything about Australia other than having studied a basic geography map of the continent. The Aborigines were people he knew nothing about. He had heard references to them, and imagined they were people who lived a life somewhere between Indians on an American reservation and the African tribes who lived in the Kalahari or the wilderness of the Kenyan countryside. The Aboriginals he saw that day lived under huts of wood and branches strewn together. Some of the families lived with their dogs under the trees. He was stunned by what he saw. Some of them looked emaciated and ill as if they desperately needed attention of the medical kind. It would be sometime before he would fully understand the nature and the conditions the Aborigines lived with.

One of them offered him something. Michael was not sure what it was and neither did he like the look of it but his mother had always taught him manners and he took it out of courtesy. Michael didn't want to be offensive so he started to eat it. It was a witchety-grub which he was longing to spit out. However he munched it and pretended that he was enjoying the taste. He smiled but it was real pretence. His stomach was churning inside.

A little while later Freddie rode up to the camp trailing Michael's horse along. Freddie had woken up and looked round for him. He was expert in matters related to bush tracking and the first thing he did was check the footprints around the billabong. It didn't take him long to work out what had happened.

Michael was sitting with a group of Aborigines eating food which he did not have a clue as to what it actually was … probably insects, grubs of some kind or the other. Freddie rode up smiling.

'I see you're learning more and more about the bush,' he growled. 'You'd better say goodbye to your new mates, we've got to get back now.'

'I'm ready to go,' Michael said.

'Come on then. Up on your horse,' Freddie said.

They both acknowledged the Aborigines and rode away. The things that Michael had seen that morning had a profound effect on him. He did not know whether it was because at the age of thirteen he had not realised people lived like this through their own choosing or if it was due to the fact that there were people in the world poorer than those he knew back home in Grenadier Guard Road.

Thirteen

Freddie and Michael made their way back to Endeavour Downs. The ride home was always easier and quicker because they had invariably mended the broken fences and rounded up the stray cattle on the outward journey.

At Endeavour Downs that morning news had come through from England. It had come all the way from Grenadier Guard Road and would await Michael when he got back to the house that evening. For years afterwards Michael would remember the impact of that day.

Roy Lane had been out checking the cattle early that day when one of the jackaroos had told him he had a message to ring the police sergeant at Broken Hill. Inside the house Josie and Doris were sweeping up. Roy went to the telephone and rang the sergeant not expecting to get the totally unprepared news..

'G'day sergeant this is Roy Lane speaking.' He stopped to listen to the policeman relay the news to him. It had come over the wire from London. His expression changed as he recognised the gravity of the news he was receiving. 'Yeah. That's right. Michael Forbes. Yes he's the young lad we've got staying with us out from England. His Aunt Doris is married to Jack Hope, our orchard manager.' A long pause followed. His face showed deep concern. He looked sideways at Doris who suddenly realised that something was terribly wrong. 'Frank Forbes! Oh gosh that is sad news.' Doris was alarmed and moved forward in expectation. She strained her ears to listen. 'What?' Roy asked. 'What was that again?' There was a slightly longer pause. 'How?' He listened attentively then turned fully to face Doris who grabbed Josie's hand instinctively out of nervousness. 'Yes. Yes. I'll tell her.' The tone of his voice sounded sombre. He replaced the receiver and looked at Doris with the expression of a man about to deliver terrible news.

'What is it Roy?' Doris asked. Her voice trembled. 'I heard you mention Frank.'

Roy looked downcast. Speaking softly he told Doris what he had just learned. It was a difficult task for him. 'Doris, I'm so sorry. I don't know how to tell you. Are you strong enough to stand what I'm going to tell you?'

A wave of panic overwhelmed Doris. 'My God. It's my brother. Oh no! Not Frank! He's dead. Isn't he?'

'I'm afraid so Doris. That was the police sergeant. He got the news over the wire.'

Josie was immediately concerned for Doris. 'We're all here for you, luv. Hang in there.'

After a while Doris found her strength within to answer. 'Yes – yes I'm fine. It's Mick I'm worried about. That young boy worshipped his Dad.' She paused to wipe a tear away. 'All my brothers gone,' she said quietly. 'Alright Roy, I'm ready. Tell me what happened. I can stand it.'

'I only really got brief details,' answered Roy. 'The sergeant was saying there's a letter to come explaining it all. But to give you a summary, apparently young Mick's father had been ill for some time.'

'I didn't know,' Doris said in all honesty.

'No it seems the bloke had been bringing up blood. He didn't tell a soul. He kept it under wraps. Anyway he was out on his air-raid warden's duties one night and then collapsed with a haemorrhage. He died that night. I'm sorry Doris. There's no easy way to tell people this kind of news.'

Doris's eyes flooded with tears. 'Oh poor Frank.' Then another thought entered her head. 'Oh, poor Honeysuckle. My goodness I've never felt the distance so much as now.'

Roy put his hand on Doris's shoulder. 'Look, don't worry about Honeysuckle. I believe some people called Spangler and Cherry are looking after her.'

That was some sort of relief at least. Through her tears Doris almost managed to smile. 'Thank God for dear old Spangler and Cherry. The old reliables.'

'Look, I've got to get back to work, Doris. Will you be alright if I leave you with Josie for now? We'll have a talk later if you need it.'

'I'll look after her Roy,' said Josie.

Roy walked to the door. He turned around before he left. 'Hang in there Doris.'

Doris tried to force another smile. She appeared to be gazing into the distance at the cattle, but in reality she was immersed in her own private feelings for Honeysuckle far away in England. Frank had gone. Her good hearted, amiable brother had gone.

It was late that night when Freddie and Michael returned to Endeavour Downs station. Unbeknown to him on the other side of the door in the main house Roy, Doris and Josie were sitting at a table drinking mugs of tea and preparing to tell Michael the shattering news about his father. He felt happy that night after his adventures on that long exhausting boundary ride. In a moment all that happiness would turn to ashes.

'They're back,' said Roy within the house. He looked out at Freddie and Michael as they led their horses away to the stables. 'The kid looks so happy too. It's going to crucify him when we give him the news.'

'We all have to live through news like this in our lifetimes,' Josie said.

'Leave it to me. I'm family, I'll look after him,' Doris said trying to ease what she considered would be a difficult situation.

'Buck up everyone,' Roy piped in. 'He'll come through. It'll be tough in the short term. We'll give him all the help and sympathy we can.'

'They're coming in now.' Josie looked round preparing everybody.

When Freddie and Michael walked into the room the atmosphere was icy. Freddie was not slow in identifying this.

'G'day everybody,' he said in his usual bright and breezy manner. He noticed everyone was silent and wore the most solemn of expressions. 'Okay folks I can see all's not well. What's wrong? Has something happened?'

Michael stood back apprehensively. Doris stood up and looked at him with an expression of deep love and sympathy. He was instinctively aware that something had happened that affected him. He felt wary and worried. Doris walked over to Michael and with a heavy heart tried to tell him as gently as possible.

'Sit down, Mick. Let's have a talk about your Dad.'

Aunt Doris did her very best to tell Michael the news without making the pain any greater than it was. He listened in disbelief and shock. The pain tore him apart inside. But that was only initially. It took many, many weeks before the full effect of what had happened truly hit Michael with all the terrifying impact he had never imagined possible. He realised with all the sadness in the world that his Dad had gone. Frank had died so suddenly and unexpectedly and he thought of that man who had never wanted for much except perhaps to make his mother and son so much happier. And of course Frank had wanted to live in Kent; the nearest place to his idea of paradise. Oh Dad, you deserved so much better, thought Michael. The pain was the worst he had ever experienced.

After that there were many times when he would ride off on his own to the solitude of a billabong. He would sit by the waters staring into space thinking of his father. He could never accept the way his father's life had ended so suddenly and cruelly when he had not been able to achieve his dreams. It seemed so unfair. Michael hoped that if there was a heaven God would find his Dad a job in one of his celestial orchards. He had never possessed strong religious faith. Yet beside those billabongs he would pray an awful lot for his father and the hope he would find the peace that on earth he was denied. He would pray also for his mum back there in the East End that she would survive.

In 1941 things began to change drastically in Australia. Menzies resigned as Prime Minister. This was followed by a short-lived premiership with Arthur Fadden at the reins. Then the Labour Leader, John Curtin, became Prime Minister. It was only a matter of time before Australia came under attack. Then Singapore fell to the Japanese and Darwin in the Northern Territory of Australia was bombed. John Curtin, a remarkably sincere and courageous man addressed the nation over the airwaves beginning his oration with the words of 'Men and women of Australia'. It was a phrase adopted by a later Australian Labour Prime Minister called Gough Whitlam but in wartime it was part of a stunning speech designed to inspire the nation in a time of crisis.

Michael was to see out the war years in the outback of Australia. After the shock of his Dad's death he immersed himself into his life there. He grew up fast. He came to know and love Australians and in particular that stalwart breed who made the bush their home.

One night Roy drove them all to a crowded cinema in a bush town where the wartime film 'The Rats of Tobruk' was showing. The stars of the film were Chips Rafferty and Peter Finch who were the forerunners of the later known Australian actors such as Rod Taylor and Jack Thompson. The film had several emotionally-charged moments which were well reflected in the looks of an audience totally transfixed. The stars of that film like Chips Rafferty on the screen in that cinema represented the 'fair dinkum' blokes and the 'dinkie die' Aussie of a bygone age. What a great people they were; full of warmth and integrity beneath that often misread brash exterior. Maybe it wasn't the sweetest of times. Maybe they weren't the happiest of times. But perhaps for Michael it was the best of times.

That same night following the main movie there was a documentary – newsreel made by the outstanding Australian cinematographer, Damien Parer. It was hardened realism of wartime images that conveyed to the audience just what their friends and relatives in uniform were enduring. Some of the scenes were quite shattering. Wounded soldiers were carried across swamps and through the jungles of Papua New Guinea. Michael looked around in the darkness of the cinema. Several women were reaching for their handkerchiefs. The scenes changed to a happier sight of Australian soldiers in slouch hats, rolling cigarettes and sporting huge grins.

Doris suddenly rose up excitedly as a familiar face graced the screen. 'It can't be!' she whispered. 'It is!' Doris couldn't have cared a fig at that moment. 'It's Jack! That's my husband Jack everybody!'

The cinema audience roared with delight. They were all on their feet yelling and cheering much to the amusement of everyone who was there. Freddie yelled out across the cinema hall, 'Oh you beaudie! Good on yer, Jack!' As an afterthought he cupped his hands together around his mouth. 'It's your shout Jack!'

Sometime later there was a dance and benefit night for soldiers at a country hall. Nobody from the station missed the opportunity to be there. Roy, Josie and their son Terry came together. Doris came along, as did Johnny and Michael. Freddie took an active role in the benefit. He compered the evening. Roy and Josie took to the dance floor. Johnny soon found himself a dancing partner. Doris preferred to help behind the tables serving out food and drink to the guests. Terry and Michael stood watching the proceedings.

Freddie was on stage with the band. He looked at bit uncomfortable but really once he was in his stride he was born for the role. The band played some rousing old dance numbers. On the dance floor there were couples enjoying the mood of the moment. There were men and women in the uniform of each of the services. Country folk in braces, shirt and tie and greasily smoothed back hair took to the dance floor with young ladies in their best Saturday night gear. Roy and Josie danced close by the table within eavesdropping distance from Terry and Michael who listened as Roy swirled Josie around. They were always extremely warm-hearted.

'I see you haven't lost your touch on the dance floor eh Roy,' Josie chuckled, her face aglow with happiness.

'It's been a while I grant you,' Roy said pulling her closer to him as they danced. 'I might be a clodhopping farmer but I'm still capable of a bit of fancy footwork.' He remembered something. 'This was how we met wasn't it?'

'Yeah. Too right it was.' Josie reminded him of more details. 'It was on a dance floor in Adelaide … '

'Woodville Town Hall to be precise,' Roy cut in quickly.

'And it was a very warm Saturday night. There was you all gawky and rambling and you couldn't dance a flaming step! You stepped all over my feet bruising them black 'n' blue. You kept telling me about the bush, the flies, the heat, the dust, the cattle. Somehow you made it all sound so damn romantic.'

'No regrets Josie? Surely!'

Josie smiled at him in that warm and wonderful way that Honeysuckle used to smile at Frank. The music ended abruptly and in the pause before the next dance Josie answered him. 'Regrets, Roy? You have to be joking. It's all been wonderful. Eventful. A lot of hardship. But my God I wouldn't have missed a single thing.'

Roy leaned across and kissed her. 'Nor me. I'd do it all again.' The music started up again and Roy whisked her away to the other side of the dance hall.

Aunt Doris and Terry joined Michael behind the table. Terry, who was about the same age as Michael, was amiable like his father Roy but at times he could be a little dogmatic. The two boys had become great mates. Aunt Doris put her arms around each of them.

'I'm proud of you boys. In a few years' time the girls will be chasing you two.'

Terry blushed with typical country-boy shyness. 'Oh geez. You make me feel embarrassed now.'

Michael wondered just where in the bush all the girls would suddenly spring from. He put Terry's mind at ease. 'I wouldn't worry if I was you Terry. There are more sheep and cattle here than there are girls.'

It brought a smile to Doris's face. 'That's true.' She sounded wistful. 'I'm glad you boys and Josie are around. It gets very lonely without Jack.'

'That's because of the war,' Terry said unthinkingly. 'That'd be right wouldn't it? You came out here and then the war started and Jack had to go away.'

'That's true. You're right though Terry. I do hope Jack gets home soon for leave. I miss him so much you know.'

Terry showed some compassion for her. 'You'll be right Doris. My Mum reckons you're a good mate to her.'

Doris was touched by this remark. In a moment of revelation she expressed her respect for Roy and Josie. 'Your Mum and Dad are two of the best, Terry. Never forget it. They've made Michael and I very welcome.'

'I won't. I reckon I've got a lot to live up to.' Terry said proudly. It was clear he loved his parents dearly. His words struck a chord with Michael. He wondered if he could ever live up to his own parents. The saddest thing of all for him was the fact that his Dad had gone and he would never know Michael as an adult. He thought of his Mum Honeysuckle. How he missed her.

The dance music came to an end once more. This time Freddie Bannan moved across to the microphone. He bathed in the spotlight. For one moment it reminded Michael of the time that Frank had occupied centre stage at the hoppers' last-night party. It would have been easy to drift away on emotional thoughts just at that minute. Luckily Freddie's warm and cheerful voice broke the spell.

'Well, ladies and gents, children and people, are you all having a bonza time?' A few people responded half-heartedly. Freddie decided to put some impetus into the evening. 'Come on everyone! Let's hear you all! Loud and clear folks! C'mon!'

This time the audience responded far more enthusiastically. 'Yeah, too right! Bonza, Freddie!'

Freddie decided to spur the audience into a fever. 'That's the way then folks! Keep your spirits up and the courage and guts that we know the Outback people have got. We've got Curtin down there in Canberra doing his damnedest to stand up for Australia! The Yanks are in the Pacific. We've got blokes like Blaney leading the troops. We've got ordinary fighting blokes over there, friends and relatives and we all wish them a speedy and safe return. But more than anything we've got ourselves as a nation. Australians are people who have always strived in adversity against every element of weather and hardship known to man. What are a few foreign attackers compared to drought, cyclone, flood and bushfire? We'll survive every time!' The audience cheered loudly and spontaneously. 'Now we really don't want to overdo it with the flag waving and the patriotism. There comes a time when we want to enjoy ourselves. Forget the traumas. Dance with someone special. Laugh! Sing! Do all the good quality things that money can't buy. Now I've got a mate down there ... '

A voice from the audience broke into Freddie's repartee. 'I didn't know you had one!' The audience laughed but it was Freddie who laughed the loudest.

He pointed to the heckler and grinned broadly. 'Now if you all want a free beer – there's the bloke who's buying!' Freddie was not to be outdone. He was always amiable but he was nobody's fool. 'Seriously,' he continued. 'Let's cut the bull for a moment. Now I do have a mate down there. No kidding! And his name's Johnny McCullough. You all know John. A bit of a local colour although he's a Jock from Glasgow originally. He's been knocking around all over the place in his life and he's one of our good mates with all the others down there at Endeavour Downs.' He then announced what was to be the highlight of the evening.

`Now John and I – we're going to give you a rendition of an old Western verse by a bloke called Robert Service. It's called *'The Shooting of Dan McGrew'*. He spun round. 'Johnny get your backside up here! Give him a round of applause!' Johnny walked through the audience smiling amid the clapping and took his place next to Freddie who chided him good naturedly. 'Look at that face! It's nostalgic to Australians. It reminds you of a battlefield where the Aussies have been!' Johnny and Freddie pretended to throw punches at each other but were joking in that peculiar Australian way of continually taking the rise. 'Have ye had a few drams then Johnny?'

'I don't know about a few drams but I'm all keyed up and ready to go. What d'ye mean I've got a face like a battlefield?'

'Good on yer mate. I'm only having a go at you!'

There were two microphones on the stage. Both were within a few feet of each other. At each one there were stools. Freddie sat down at one and adjusted one microphone to his level. Johnny did exactly the same. They had been practising this routine for weeks. As if on cue the two men winked at each other. Freddie snapped his fingers and almost in immediate response the curtain on the stage drew back.

On the stage behind Freddie and Johnny were people dressed up like something out of the Wild West. The setting was supposed to be an old-time saloon. There were cowboys playing cards and a small slight man with a hat miles too big for his head. He was portraying Dangerous Dan McGrew, one of the central characters of Robert Service's famous verse. Towering above him was a voluptuous heavily made-up saloon girl resembling the film star Mae West. This was the famous 'Lady that's known as Lou'. When Freddie and Johnny delivered their verses alternately the drama comedy unfolded on the stage behind them. The people in the audience were already boosted up in spirit by Freddie's early performance and they relaxed as the two men on stage performed in a vaudevillian manner.

Freddie began in a low hushed voice. 'Ladies and gentlemen …' He paused and spoke in a louder emphatic voice. *'The Shooting of Dan McGrew.'*

Michael settled back behind the tables of food and watched Freddie and Johnny give a recitation in an expressive and mischievous manner.

> *'A bunch of the boys were whooping it up in the Malamute saloon;*
> *The kid that handles the music box was hitting a rag-time tune,*
> *Back of the bar, in a solo game, sat Dangerous Dan McGrew,*
> *And watching his luck was his light-o'-Love, the Lady that's known as Lou.'*
> *Johnny came in on the second verse. His dour expression exploded into one*
>   *of twinkling mischief.*
> *'When out of the night, which was fifty below, and into the dire and the glare,*
> *There stumbled a miner fresh from the creeks, dog-dirty and loaded for bear.*
> *He looked like a man with a foot in the grave, and scarcely the strength of a Louse,*
> *Yet he tilted a poke of dust on the bar and he called for drinks for the house.*
> *There was none could place the stranger's face, though we searched ourselves*
>   *for a clue,*
> *But we drank his health, and the last to drink was Dangerous Dan McGrew.'*

At the conclusion of many verses the audience were on their feet giving Johnny and Freddie a standing ovation.

It was at that benefit night that Roy was introduced to a Government Minister who had come up from Canberra for the occasion. He was the Member of Parliament for the area and Endeavour Downs was slap bang in the middle of his constituency. Michael did not know what was said between the two men. But the following day when Terry and Michael were riding with the drovers, Roy was asking everyone to make a tally count of all the cattle. He was shortly to find out the reason for this.

Fourteen

Roy asked everyone at Endeavour Downs to attend a meeting in the drovers' hut. With most of the staff away at war there was a curious bunch in attendance. Apart from Michael there was Terry, Johnny, Josie, Freddie, Doris and two other drovers – Joe, a permanently smiling Aborigine, and a fellow in his early twenties called Don Jones who was a skilled horseman. They knew that Don would be leaving shortly to join the services. The whole station was being maintained by the most threadbare of staff. Everyone sat in anticipation of what Roy was about to tell them.

'You're probably wondering why I've got you all here tonight.' He smiled at them all. 'Don't worry, I'm not going to sack any of you! Strewth! That would leave the whole show for me to run. I'm looking at all of you folk and you are the staff! The other blokes are at war. Well the reason I've got you all here tonight is that the other night at the benefit the local member was there with one of the big boys from Canberra.'

'Canberra!' exclaimed Freddie looking perturbed. 'You don't know something we don't, do you Roy?'

Roy took on a serious expression. 'That's just it. I do. We all know the state of play as far as the war has gone here in Australia. Darwin took a panning. Battles have been rife in New Guinea and the Pacific. Jap subs even emerged in Sydney Harbour. Well, if there's a Jap invasion from up north working its way down from New Guinea through the territories and into Queensland or even down here – it's only a possibility mind, just speculation at this stage and don't get me wrong, there will be a lot of invading soldiers with hungry bellies. Hungry for our beef. Good ol' Aussie beef. So this bloke was telling me, for the country's sake, to get the lot shifted to Southern Queensland. We're not feeding the enemy?'

'You want us to move all of them boss?' queried the Aboriginal drover Joe. 'We've only a few here.'

It was the turn of the normally quiet drover, Don Jones, to say something. 'And a few thousand head of cattle, Roy. What's this leading up to?'

'Let me guess,' pondered Freddie. 'You, me, our three mates here. All of us droving a few thousand head. You've got to be joking.'

'Why not?' asked Roy. He let the question sink in. 'It's not widely talked about for obvious reasons but one of the biggest cattle drives in our history has just taken place. One hundred-thousand big, noisy beef cattle have been shifted by barely a couple of dozen people from the Northern Territory to Queensland. A couple of dozen people! Imagine that everybody, including women and children!' He stopped and looked around the room. 'Okay then Ladies and Gents, we're going to move a few thousand cattle. I'm going. I know that much. It's going to be a bit lonely on my own. Anyone want to come along?' He announced the route of the cattle drive with a sense of real pride. 'From Endeavour Downs, New South Wales to Ogilvie Junction, Queensland. What a trip!'

Everyone in the room looked to be shocked at first. Josie smiled slightly. Roy had obviously confided in her earlier. Johnny rubbed his chin and contemplated what he had just heard. Freddie looked at the other drovers to see if anyone else was volunteering. He leaned forward on his chair which squeaked slightly.

'Why not?' he drawled in a casual manner. 'Yes, I'll come along to keep you out of mischief. Wasn't doing anything much anyway. Beats sitting on my backside.'

Roy laughed gently at Freddie's response. He knew Freddie too well to be taken in by his apparent lack of enthusiasm. The onlookers suspected what Roy probably knew anyway. Freddie was thrilled to his boot heels at the mouth-watering prospect of an overland cattle drive to Queensland.

'So there's two of us now,' Roy said with a touch of relish. 'That makes the job a little easier for me.' He looked across at Johnny almost daring him to come along. 'How about it John? We need a bloke to drive a wagon with food and stores in. Will you have a go?'

'Me!' He seemed genuinely astonished to be asked. 'I'm an odd job man. I'd be a bit long in the tooth for this. Surely?'

'You're no older than you want to be. Will you come? We need you.' Then he made what sounded like a plea, more than a request. 'Would you do it for a mate? There's only us lot left.'

A warm smile spread across his grizzled face which in some ways was like a contour map of lines. 'Now you put it like that Roy. Why not? Besides, I've never been to Ogilvie Junction. And ye' never know what young Freddie here is going to get up to. I'm in. Why not? It's another experience.'

'And you'll need a cook.' Doris volunteered without any prompting. 'I can ride Roy. You know that.'

Roy was delighted. 'That's the shot Doris. Josie's going.' He winked at her flirtatiously. 'Aren't you darl?' Between the two of you, I reckon we'll have a few good meals. Our boy Terry will be coming. What about your nephew Michael? Do you think he'll come?'

'Of course he will!' Johnny remarked sharply.

'He'll come,' Doris said with certainty and she looked across at Michael. He nodded and smiled. A cattle drive! At the age of sixteen – it was hard to believe so much had happened to him in three years.

Roy summed up the situation so far. 'How are we going then? There's me, John, Freddie, Doris, Josie, Mick, Terry.' He turned to the other two remaining drovers. 'Now what about you blokes? I know you two are new to this station but we need every bit of help we can get.'

'I come along Boss. Might be a good ride.' Joe the Aborigine seemed eager.

'Yeah. I wouldn't miss it for the world,' said Don.

Roy was pleased. His gentle cajoling had got everybody to volunteer for the cattle drive. 'We leave the day after tomorrow at first light.'

Josie stood up and proudly said, 'It's good to know that us women haven't been left out eh Doris? We'll be battling our way as good as the blokes.'

'Eight of us, men, women and children droving thousands of cattle. I would never have believed it.' Doris smiled at Roy.

Roy grinned. 'And neither would I. Who would have dreamed it? We've got a couple of locals who are going to run the station while we're away. The rest of us, plus anyone we pick up on the way, are going to try and pull off the impossible.' For a moment Roy looked worried. He looked to the ceiling as if he was seeking divine inspiration. 'By God, we're going to pull through this one!' he added determinedly.

★★★

The cattle drive was without a doubt the greatest memory of Michael's years in the Australian bush. He was then sixteen and the impression it made was so vivid that for years afterwards he would smell and sense it all if he reflected on that time. They were strong and powerful memories of cattle herds, dust and heat, but more strongly of friendships forged from solitude.

Roy was in charge without laying the law down to anybody. People respected him. He did not command. He did not delegate. Roy's simple rule in life was to lead and set the example. He rode alongside the huge herd constantly keeping check of the situation. Don and Joe rode around the herds maintaining the lines. Doris and Josie also rode in much the same manner watching out for strays who might decide to wander away. Johnny had a ringside seat observing from the interior of the covered wagon. Every so often Freddie would ride back to see how he was getting on.

Michael rode with Terry who was a fearless horse rider. He was full of zest and spirit. Sometimes his enthusiasm would run away with him. Michael held back on these occasions. Aunt Doris was also reticent. In truth, they were a little nervous. The sheer size of the herd was overpowering. The horses could react in sharp ways sometimes. The thought of being thrown always made Michael take every care that his horse never got out of control.

Occasionally, Josie would ride up to her husband and the two of them would watch the herd stream past over rugged bushland.

Don and Joe were men born for this type of life. They were excellent riders who rode in a breathtaking, devil-may-care attitude. Joe would ride as if there was no tomorrow. He enjoyed every bit of his tough and enduring work. Don always seemed so cheerful and enthusiastic. They loved their work. Perhaps that was the key to their perpetual energy.

It was surprising just how well Doris and Josie fitted into this cattle drive. They were both women in their thirties. In bush outfits they did not lose their natural feminine attractiveness in any way. They rode up and down keeping control of the herds with as much vigour as the men they were accompanying. Doris removed her hat from time to time smoothing her hair back. Somehow she always managed to look sparkling in spite of the discomforts of the desert. It was only the red dust on her face that indicated her own struggle against the climate.

One of the most wonderful sights Michael would remember was the night falling as the cattle sped through the bush. It was a sight worthy of a great artist's work. The shadowy silhouettes of the drivers blended against the deep red of the sky, the shades of the cattle in brown and auburn against the backdrop of golden red iridescent earth and glowing luminous trees.

At camp the breathing space was welcome. Always on these nights it was a time for Michael to gain insight into some of the characters he rode with. It was always like a scene from one of those American Western movies except it was happening to him and this was not Monument Valley or Hollywood but the Australian Outback. Sometimes these campfire nights could be revealing for the people he met spoke their true feelings to one another in confidence, in a way that one could never do in the city.

He rarely heard Joe and Don talk much. They were private people. Perhaps a little shy, he thought. Maybe even not given to talking at the best of times. By no means a fault of course, but one night Michael heard Joe speak openly in a way he had not thought possible.

There were remnants of a fire burning. Freddie lit up his cigarette, the sparkle of the flame igniting bright in the dark. He lay back on his sleeping bag blowing the occasional ring of smoke into the air and gazed into the magnificent wide sky. Johnny wandered over and hard a yarn to him. A few yards away Terry and Michael lay on their blanket rolls. Doris, Josie and Roy were chatting to each other by the campfire.

Michael watched as Don and Joe sat beneath a tree a little way from the camp. Joe had been alone and appeared to be troubled. Don had noticed this and went across to see him. Even though they spoke quietly the words drifted back to where Michael was laying.

'What's up cobber?' Don gently asked.

Joe looked up. His red streaked eyes looked moist. It seemed he was on the verge of tears. Joe was slow in replying. He tapped the back of the coolibah tree as if it was a long-lost relative or friend.

'Something wrong, Joe?' Don asked, perturbed his first question hadn't got a reply.

'This tree.' It was a strange answer. Don winched his eyebrows. 'This tree,' said Joe. Michael was curious and listened intently.

'I don't understand you mate,' Don said, rolling a cigarette.

There was a silence as Don waited for Joe to say something. It was broken as Joe spoke for the longest time Michael had ever heard him speak.

'My mother gave birth to me under this tree,' Joe said in sad melancholic tones. 'She died under this tree.' Don could not say anything.

He could only look on and listen sympathetically. 'Yeah, sitting under this tree brings me closer to my family I guess. I haven't been here for sometime now. I feel my mother's spirit is here. Funny sort of a place to call home, isn't it Don?'

Don looked at the tree and ran his hand over the trunk. 'Seems pretty firm and strong to me Joe.'

Joe slowly responded. 'Old tree was there before I was born. Reckon this old tree will be standing long and tall after I'm gone. My mother gave birth to my brothers under this tree. All gone now, Don.' There was a silence. Michael was sure from where he lay that he saw Joe tremble and rest his head in his hands. Don put his hand on Joe's shoulder. 'I like to stay alone for a while now.'

'Sure mate. This is your place Joe. Maybe it's just a tree in the scrub to some. But the way I look at it this earth and the roots of this fine old tree, it's not just a piece of bark, it's a shrine, a place of worship.' Don considered his words. 'This is a place you can come to and you can feel the closeness of your family. It's not something made of bricks and concrete. It's a living thing mate.' He slapped the tree trunk. 'While this tree keeps on growing, your family will always be with you.'

Joe lowered his head. 'True. Something else Don ...'

'What's that, cob?'

'This is my family's heartbeat. All buried here.'

Don looked thunderstruck. He was totally lost for words when he realised that this particular spot in the bush really was a shrine. Don half smiled and walked away leaving Joe to his own private memories.

Michael looked away aware this was something personal to Joe. He did not want to be intrusive and rolled over with the intention of trying to sleep. Terry's voice rung in his ears suddenly from a few feet away.

'What are you going to do when the war's over Mick? Are you going to stay here? Go back maybe to England?'

He sat up and faced him. 'I'll go home for sure,' he said with an air of certainty. 'Definitely. I miss my Mum. I do miss home.'

Terry was deeply interested. 'What was it like? Your home?'

'Where I used to live you mean?' Terry nodded. 'I used to live with my Mum and Dad in a few rooms in a terraced house. Most of the families round our way lived in them. It was a bit of a rough area. Lots of factories. Lots of fights and gangs. Didn't look too good either. Even this lot looks brighter compared to my street.' Michael thought hard about it for a moment. 'But it was my home. I miss my mother. All the people I knew. I've been here nearly three years now.' He then revealed something he had been keeping bottled up within for a long time. 'I miss my Dad. I miss him so much. But he's never coming back. He's gone forever.'

Terry tried to be kind. 'You've got us mate. I know it's not the same. But we're all your mates. My Dad and Mum, Johnny, Freddie, Jack, Doris. We're almost all family.'

'Don't get me wrong, Terry. I've enjoyed it here and I really like everybody. But I need my home. With my Dad gone my Mum's going to need support and help. She's on her own over there. And I'm out here.'

'I understand. What about Doris? Do you think she'll go home too? That's if Jack doesn't come through. They reckon a lot of Aussies, from the same bunch of troops that Jack's in, are in prisoner-of-war camps in the Far East. There's been no word on Jack for a long while. Doris has been real quiet with us blokes around but by geez, she's been pouring her heart out to Mum and Dad each night. I tell you Mick, she's been in floods of tears every night.'

Michael was obviously shocked by what he had just heard. He could not believe his Aunt Doris had not confided in him. 'I never knew.' He gazed hard at Terry.

Terry noticed Michael's dismay. 'I don't think she wanted you to get worried. You losing your Dad was a pretty big blow to her as well, mate. Maybe you could grab a few words with her out on the trail tomorrow. I'm sorry I told you. I'm big with my mouth sometimes.'

'Don't be,' Michael said trying not to show how hurt he was at Doris's secret. 'I know now.'

He looked across to where his Aunt Doris was sitting with Roy and Josie and studied Doris's face for signs of the deep worry she was obviously concealing. There was nothing on the surface. At this point Joe, fresh from his melancholy moments beneath the coolibah tree joined the others. Don sat down with them as well. Michael turned away and rolled over. This time he would sleep. That was what he thought. He found himself looking in the direction of Freddie and Johnny. These two men were fascinating characters in themselves. Michael didn't eavesdrop. He listened because he knew he was being downright nosey and they were so interesting in the way they spoke.

The cattle were resting in the background. The light from the moon was glowing brightly and beams flickered through the gleaming gums in the dark purple bush sky. Johnny sat on a packing case sipping from a mug while Freddie lay back chain smoking.

'I know mate,' Freddie began, 'I reckon you and I, in our own separate individual ways were born for this, a cattle drive over some of the most spectacular and rugged land that God ever created. Nights of the longest silences a bloke could ever wish to hear. Moments of splendour, moments of glory on a horse behind a herd. It's a great feeling.'

'The Outback seems to breed a dreamy quality in people.' Johnny spoke in the manner of a man who could never be lost for words. 'The sea did that for me. I loved listening to the sounds of the waves and the wind, and seeing the stars sparkle over the ocean at night. We must have similar Celtic blood in us Freddie old mate.'

'I've got some Scottish blood in my ancestral line. A touch or two of Irish. That's where I get the blarney from. A real mixture of intermarriage back in the ages. I'm the last in my line. The last of the Bannans.'

'You've got a touch of the poet about you. That's the Scot in you. You're the boundary rider that quotes Byron and Shelley and Shakespeare to the dingoes and the trees.'

'And you're the bloke that writes that sort of stuff,' Freddie responded in a jocular manner.

'Melancholy times bring that out in me,' said Johnny.

'Like when you're thinking of your home in Scotland I guess. You haven't been home since – how long has it been John?'

'Since 1919,' Johnny stated clearly, 'and now it's 1943. I wrote a poem a few nights ago about it. Would it embarrass you if I read it to you Freddie?'

'Wouldn't embarrass me, John. You know that. Go for your life.'

Johnny reached into a bag and took out a couple of sheets of paper on which his poem was written. Unbeknown to him he had a captive audience. The others, aware that Johnny was about to read out loud, turned to listen.

'Are you sure I won't embarrass you reading this?' he asked again.

'No,' Freddie replied. 'I'm sentimental really. Words of a gentle kind of nature can bring a tear to my eye. I know it's not a manly thing to cry and few tough old bushies might laugh their breeches off but I reckon good poetry, or even a sensitive letter from someone who means something special to you can be very moving.'

'I know what you mean. Well I wrote this when I was thinking of a time I was stuck in a North of England town when I couldn't get home for leave from the Navy. The other night I thought of my home and I wrote this poem.' He drew a breath. 'This poem I entitled '*The Lochs and The Heather.*'

There was a sudden silence. Johnny began to speak and Michael had never heard poetry spoken so beautifully in such an unusual setting.

'Far, far away from the sweet smelling air of the Highlands and the tones of bagpipes plaintive on the air,

A Scotsman rises in his lonely room in a smoky city in the midst of squalid tenements with a view of huge grey monoliths for scenery and industrial factories everywhere.

How far away now are the lochs and the heather as is the crisp, bracing, clean fine air and the vivid scenic colours.

Memories of hard gruelling work in the shipyards of the Clyde cannot erase the pleasure of life in that green land.

Which spawned the likes of many tartaned clans and great literary names such as Robert Louis Stevenson and the immortal Robbie Burns.

Such colours in those quaint fishing villages and in the shimmering of the lochs of Fyne, Lomond and Ness.

Sheep herding in the Highlands, the toughness of the Grampian to the character of Strathclyde.

A Scotsman drinking in a crowded lonely bar, many miles away, recalls his youthful life through a haze of frivolity and drink.

Yet the haze is clearing and beyond the mist he can view the Western Isles.

But it is not the sound of glasses clinking or the low buzz of pub talk that he hears,

It is the steady beat of pipe and drum played by the kilted marching men in pageantry at a military tattoo.

Scotland the Brave from whence he came, to there he'll remain patriotic, proud and true.

Prosaic beauty in the fall of autumn leaves, bare brown trees, faded rugged grass,

Winter winds, chilly night, snow upon the Highlands, and warm cosy log fires burning, snug at night,

New Year's Eve, haggis on the table, family kilted, laughing, smiling in an old stone house; there are celebrations tonight,

Then the haze clears yet again, tears trickle down a lonely Scotsman's face,
he gazes deep into his glass,
He's in a crowded lonely bar on New Year's Eve and he's not really home
tonight,
The Scotsman's far away from the time of his youth and the land of the lochs
and the heather.'

There was a marvellous atmosphere in the bush after Johnny had spoken the words of his poem. It was hard to describe the feeling that existed then. Freddie smiled gently and blew a ring of cigarette smoke that spiralled upwards in the lustrous darkness. Michael too smiled for he had enjoyed the emotive way Johnny always expressed himself.

'Nice John,' Freddie finally said. 'Makes me homesick for a place I've never been.'

Close by, Doris turned to Josie, who made an observing remark.

'Bet you didn't know that Johnny had such a soft heart eh, Doris?'

'He's a surprise package,' Doris agreed. 'The last time I heard a poem like that was when I came over on the boat, and a man called Ben Daneman read one about Australia he'd written.'

She smiled at the memory of it. Doris looked around at the drovers' camp and Michael suspected she was still thinking how amazing it was to actually be there in the middle of the bush.

Fifteen

The group of drovers stirred in the early morning sunrise. Roy was already up and he stood looking at the great red sun rising on the horizon line. Already the cattle were getting restless; a sure sign it was time to start moving again.

They were soon on the move travelling over the ever-changing contours of this land. Michael thought that Australia must have had every conceivable colour in the texture of the land. The cattle passed over plains, hills, ridges and scrub with spartan vegetation. The river crossing was the most difficult.

Several hundred cattle streamed into the waters of a fast flowing river while the rest of the herd accumulated behind. Don and Joe who knew no fear were the first drovers to enter the water on their horses closely followed by Roy. The flow of the river was strong although the water was not too deep. Somehow, despite the fiercely strong river flow, the drovers managed to keep the cattle going across from one side to the other.

It was a hard job to control the herd. Much of the cattle were hesitant to enter the waters. Freddie cracked his stockwhip hard on the ground diverting any strays back to the mainstream of the cattle herd. Terry and Michael eagerly awaited a sign from Roy to come across. Behind them were grouped Josie and Doris, and Johnny in the cook's wagonette.

On the other side Roy removed his hat and waved it, indicating to the drovers to come across. 'Bring them over folks!' he called out high spiritedly. 'Bring the best beef in the world over!'

In response, Terry and Michael immediately started forward and whip-cracked the ground. The cattle began to move forward steadily into the water. They rode to the water's edge and waited for a moment or so. Josie had no such reservations. She rode forward in a game and plucky fashion making sure that the herd did not separate. Doris, Terry and Michael followed on quickly. They made it to the other side much to Roy's delight.

Roy turned to Don and Joe. 'Don, I want to keep count of these boys as they come in. How d'you reckon you'd go on tallying?'

'Me! Oh my word!' Don was surprised. 'Well I generally get the count pretty close. Give or take a few.'

'Okay Don. Count the beggars. What about you Joe?'

'I can't count Boss,' Joe said shyly. 'I can keep an eye on the cattle though.'

Roy was very embarrassed. 'Should have thought of that shouldn't I? Alright Don, there will be no second count. Try and tally as close as you can. Joe, keep an eye on the cattle. Make sure none of them start wandering off.'

'Will do. No problem.' Joe swung into action and rode off after some strays.

Johnny took his wagonette into the river. Michael rode with Doris, Terry and Freddie controlling the herd. Don counted the animals keenly watching every one of them. It was a busy scene with all hands active. Eventually all the cattle were accounted for. It was soon back to dry land and the drive continued across the plain.

Roy rode across to Don who was counting the last few cattle. The dust column continued to rise as the herd moved into the distance.

'How did you go mate?'

Don answered with a question. 'Before we left did you do a tally yourself?'

'I certainly did. Don't let me down mate. Tell me a figure close to my own.'

'I don't know how many you got Roy,' he looked concerned. 'My figure is – try 2,241.'

Roy gave an appearance of being astonished. '2,241?'

'Yeah that's right,' Don replied almost defensively. 'I was a bit worried. Back at Endeavour Downs you mentioned a few thousand. I didn't miscount. I know that for sure.'

Roy broke into a laughing smile. 'No I'm only playing around. You're close enough. But Don … down the track we'll be picking up another 3,000 at the Conmee Homestead. And probably half a dozen more drovers.'

Don gaped in amazement. 'Nearly 5,500, eh! It's going to be interesting.'

The days on the cattle drive were long. There was so much distance to be covered and so little time to achieve it all in. Freddie constantly checked on the herd. He would ride back to see Johnny who handled the wagonette with skill. It was late into the night and Freddie rode back to the wagon, tied his horse to it and got inside. Freddie was always amused by his mates' dour expressions which revealed little. Johnny on the other hand found Freddie's laconic humour to be rib-tickling.

'You must feel like you're in Cobb and Co or something,' Freddie said to Johnny referring to those stagecoach drivers of another era who travelled the length and breadth of Australia.

'Who talked me into this then? Am I adventurous or mad?' Johnny retorted in good humour.

'Ah come on mate. It's not that bad. You love it really! Besides, we're going to stop off at the Conmee's place at Culgabra Creek. Warm beds. A decent night's sleep. Jim and Mickie Conmee are terrific hosts.'

'I can do with that I can tell you!' Johnny laughed. 'I haven't had a decent night's sleep since I left. Have you ever really thought about what this ride is all about? I mean, I'm not a drover. That's your line of business. But I'm sitting here observing the whole thing. For one eternity of a long day – every day – we're behind the mob. And we seem to carry out a routine of sorts.'

'What do you mean Johnny?'

'We ride. We smoke. We canter or suddenly we splurge into great bursts of enthusiasm. We get covered in dirt and red dust and earth flying up from the cattle hoofs. Sometimes the cattle are slow. They're moody like people in that respect. And sometimes the damned creatures rear up and act as if they're possessed by old man Satan himself. They spark and stampede as if an electricity bolt has been hurtled at them. At night we sleep in our blanket rolls trying to close our eyes and if sleep won't come, we count the stars splintering across the sky or listen to the beasts murmuring all night long. It's a hell of a life.'

Terry and Michael were riding just by the wagon and listened to the two men's voices drifting in the night air.

'That's droving mate,' Freddie replied in response to Johnny's ever eloquent utterances. 'That's the hard and fast of it all. When I told my Dad I was leaving a safe bank job in Adelaide, giving up the rush of King William Street to go jackarooing in the bush, he reckoned I'd gone out of my head. Still reckon it was one of the best things I ever did. Its been a good life. I wouldn't have missed this for all the world.'

Johnny broke into a smile. 'Neither would I! But, by God, it's rough.'

'Just think of it, Jock,' Freddie reminded him. 'Tomorrow night we'll be at old Jimmy Conmee's place at Culgabra. We'll be in good company. Nice beds. Cold beer. Plenty of good tucker.' He leaned out of the wagon because he knew Terry and Michael were riding close by. 'How does that sound young Michael?'

'I'm hungry already,' Michael replied.

'Absolutely bonza,' said Terry.

★★★

They really did make the most of that short stay when the group of drovers arrived at the Conmee's homestead. In good company and freshly washed, everyone was in a sparkling mood. Especially Freddie who started singing *The Wild Colonial Boy*. Soon everybody joined in. Josie was on the piano. Doris, Roy and Johnny backed Freddie up in the singing. Freddie prompted Terry and Michael to join in on the sing-song. Jim and Micheline Conmee, the elderly homestead owners were a generous couple full of good spirit who made sure everyone had something to eat. Don and Joe preferred to sit outside but the Conmees went out several times to give them a good helping of food.

While the others were laughing, singing and drinking, Michael saw his Aunt Doris take a glass of beer and walk out onto the verandah. He followed her. She stood looking at the stars and then sat down. Michael had wanted to speak to her since Terry had told him his Uncle Jack was a POW. From within there was singing as the little group broke into a series of old songs. Doris looked up at Michael as he approached.

'Reminds me of those old sing-a-long nights at Grenadier Guard Road,' she said.

Michael sat down beside his aunt and wondered how he could broach the subject cautiously. 'Funny, I was just thinking the same thing,' said Michael as he risked bringing the subject up. 'Aunt Doris, why are you out here? I know you've been talking a lot to Josie and Roy.'

'Do you know what I'm thinking then?' she asked.

'Yes,' he answered softly and cautiously. 'You're thinking about Uncle

Jack and where he is at the moment.' Aunt Doris looked alarmed for a moment then her expression slowly changed to one of relief. Michael tried to offer some comforting words. 'It's alright. I'm only sixteen but I'm not silly. I know you've been upset.'

Doris looked at him aware he was more sensitive than she realised. She was probably glad to be able to talk about it. 'Jack's in a prisoner-of-war camp somewhere in the Far East you know. I wish I knew how he was. There are some terrible stories coming back.' Doris was calm and reserved as she spoke but there was agony in her eyes. After a pause she continued. 'They are talking about the railroad in Burma. There are a lot of British and Australian servicemen working on it.' Her voice faltered slightly. 'I find it hard to talk about.'

'I understand,' Michael said with emphasis. 'Really I do. It could all be over in a year or two.'

Doris took a different view. 'I'll believe that when it happens. The fact that cattle stations all over Australia are moving their herds across should indicate that the Government still takes the threat of invasion seriously enough.'

'We're going to be on the move again tomorrow,' said Michael. 'Some 5,000 cattle altogether Roy reckons. And a few more drovers to help us.' From behind, Josie walked on to the verandah followed by Mr and Mrs Conmee. 'Should be a great show.'

Josie joined them. 'It certainly should, young Michael,' she reiterated. 'Now there's a bonza ding-dong going on in there. Johnny, Roy and Freddie are singing their hearts out.'

'I might stay out here if you don't mind Josie,' said Doris.

Jim Conmee affably made himself present. 'Would you mind if me and the missus joined you? It's not often we get the chance to talk to many people passing through.'

Doris conceded with a gentle smile. 'Oh, why not?' Mr and Mrs Conmee and Josie sat down with them. 'It'll do me good. I was feeling a bit down.'

'Why's that?' Jim asked. 'Are you worried about something?'

'My husband's away at war. He's a POW somewhere. My family, apart from my nephew Michael here, are in England. My brother died when he was out on duty as an air raid warden. The rest of the family survived the Blitz. Only just though.'

Mrs Conmee looked concerned. 'It's a bit of a worry isn't it? And you say your husband's a POW?' Doris nodded in reply. 'By geez, it's a rough road for some eh, Jim?'

'Yeah that's for sure,' Jim agreed. 'These are trying times for a lot of us. I know it might be a far road down the track but when's it's all over there'll be parties all over Australia. The people had it rough with the Depression. Then they had the war. When it's all over the people are going to be so tough, very little will be able to hurt them anymore. I reckon you'd feel that way wouldn't you now?'

'Oh time will tell I guess,' Doris said matter-of-factly.

Mrs Conmee turned to Michael. 'What about you young fellow? What's all this meant to you?'

He contemplated his answer. 'I can't believe I'm here. So many things seem to have happened the past few years. From where I used to live, to coming out here and being on a cattle drive. I can't believe it. I was at home with my Mum and Dad in London. We lived in a couple of rooms. Bath night was Friday. We used the same water after each other. We used the same towel. We used to go hop-picking in Kent and I thought the countryside was big there. But this is so big. And so empty.'

'Make the most of it young lad,' said Mrs Conmee. 'You'll look back on these times all your life.'

Jim agreed. 'That's true y'know. Some of the toughest and roughest times in life – well I think they take on a bit of an afterglow.'

The small group sat in silence for a moment or two sipping drinks. Up above the sky was almost crimson in colour. The cattle were making plenty of noise. In the house the party was in full swing. Johnny, Freddie, Roy and Don who had joined them were singing *Mademoiselle from Armentieres*' at the top of their voices.

Jim laughed quietly to himself. 'Haven't heard that since last Anzac Day.'

Mrs Conmee remarked on it. 'Yeah some of the boys here were in the last war. We always make a point of breaking out the beer and the cucumber sandwiches on that day. We hold a Remembrance Service too. A lot of the blokes round here joined up. A lot of them never made it back. We don't forget our mates who died.'

'And we never do,' said Jim.

Josie came back into the conversation. 'Freddie was a soldier in the last one. He was on the Somme. Johnny was a sailor. Had a pretty rough time of it too.'

Almost on cue, Freddie appeared on the verandah looking happy and boisterous. He was simply bubbling over with enthusiasm.

'Come on everybody!' he shouted. 'We're moving out 5,000 cattle tomorrow. There'll be thirty of us now. New drovers. C'mon let's have a ripper sing-song.'

In the background they could hear Johnny singing *A wee doch and Doris*. Aunt Doris stood up decided her period of reflective thinking was over. 'What about it then?' she asked.

'That's the way love,' said Jim.

They needed no further prompting. They all entered the room and joined in the singing. Through the window Michael saw Joe the Aboriginal drover peer from outside. He smiled broadly. Michael wondered if he would have joined them if he had been asked but nobody thought to do so.

Sixteen

There was now a herd of a full 5,000 cattle. The drovers' strength had increased to thirty. Johnny had swapped his wagon to ride as a drover. The ride was a great deal easier now. They crossed salt bush plains and ascended hills without too much difficulty. The skill of the new drovers was something to watch.

The most difficult part of the journey was on the open plains particularly when the sun was at its highest and the intense heat took its toll on the group of riders. In the middle of the afternoon it conjured up images of how a Foreign Legionnaire or an intrepid colonial explorer must have felt when faced with the full blast of a desert sun.

One of these days was to prove fatal. It was the most tepid afternoon Michael had ever endured. Roy removed his hat and wiped his forehead. His face was full of beads of perspiration. Johnny was struggling to keep his eyes open. Michael was half asleep on his horse. Terry was dangerously close to falling off his horse until Michael prodded him from his slow doze. Roy turned around and looked at the group with concern. He noticed Freddie riding slowly.

'Are you alright there Freddie?' Roy called out.

'Hot mate. And it's getting hotter,' Freddie called back wiping his eyes.

Roy smiled back at him and shielded his eyes from the sun. Up there in the sky the sun hung there almost like a glittering lantern. Even the cattle were slowing down. Joe was the only one who was really alert. He rode up and down keeping the cattle in check.

Freddie turned around and rode to where Johnny was riding slowly. 'How goes it Johnny? Bet you wished you'd stayed in the shade of the cook's wagonette?'

Johnny eked out a tiny smile. 'I can stand it – just.' He broke out into one of his lyrical passages. 'I would just love to see the cool flow of waters. Some bubbling springs with lovely frothy waters. Green grass and a cool breeze.'

If anyone else had spoken these words Michael felt sure they would have been dismissed as being either a crackpot or a waffler. Johnny had the capacity to speak long flowing passages and yet never lose sight of his sense of romance nor his sincerity.

'You'd have to go back to your homeland for that,' said Freddie. 'This is Queensland, mate. It's a wonderful state too. Won't be long before it's all over and we'll be on our way back to Endeavour Downs. Tough going but it's worth it. There's a waterhole a few miles ahead.'

Johnny gazed at the cattle. 'We're going to have a lot of thirsty beasts here.'

Freddie allowed himself some rough-hewn humour. 'Forget about the drovers mate! The cattle are dying for a drink too!' Johnny grinned. 'I'm going to check on the others, Jock.'

Above the herd a couple of birds flew in the direction of the waterhole. Michael wondered just what the view of the herd must have seemed from up above. To be riding with 5,000 cattle was an awe-inspiring experience. He did notice one thing. The pace of the herd was beginning to quicken. He was not the only one to notice this.

Don was something of a loner. He remained studiously detached, always keeping his own station. He watched intently as the lazy pace of the herd seemed to be gathering momentum. Don had a habit he perpetually carried out. He would roll a cigarette down his trouser leg and then toss it in the air catching it in his lips. He was well practised but as he performed this habit he lit the cigarette and stared down at the pace of the cattle. His expression showed concern for he realised that the herd had smelt water and that they were building up for a stampede.

This sudden rapid pace was not unnoticed by Johnny. He gripped the reins tightly almost in alarm. He looked towards Roy at the head of the herd.

All of the drovers reacted in different ways. Some looked shocked. Others appeared hesitant as to what to do. Joe as always feared nothing. He rode hard down towards the front of the herd. Other drovers reached for their stockwhips and cracked the ground hard to try and keep control. It set a precedent. Suddenly, everyone seemed to be hitting the ground with their stockwhips.

It was too late. The herd accelerated fast. They were diversifying and spreading out in all different directions. Doris and Josie at one side of the drive looked on aghast at the stampede.

'What's happening?' Doris gasped in shock.

'The beasts can smell the waterhole.' Josie looked panic-stricken. 'We've gotta go, Dot. The boys are going to have a job rounding them up. Let's go, Doris!'

The two women immediately rode off in pursuit of the cattle. It was a terrifying sight with the cattle bearing down in full force. Everyone in the droving team rode down hard in a bid to circumvent the stampede. Freddie had the same look of intent as everybody else but he was driving himself much harder. Dangerously harder.

Roy rode up to the top of a rock ridge to head off one line of cattle. He diverted them back down in a single handed manner of furious riding.

Freddie raced away after a single line of cattle. He seemed to disappear in a cloud of dust somewhere.

To Michael's horror he suddenly found himself caught in the middle of stampeding cattle all around him. His horse reared up suddenly almost throwing him off. He desperately hung on for dear life as the cattle ran around him.

Luckily close by, Terry saw Michael's plight. Using his extraordinary skills of horsemanship Terry ploughed his way through to where Michael was surrounded. He was surprised at Terry's courage as he leapt onto the ground and turned to face the oncoming herd. He grabbed his stockwhip and struck at the ground in several places. He yelled and screamed at the cattle. He jumped up and down. The cattle began to separate and scatter. In a remarkable display of tenacity Terry faced the cattle head on. His eyes moved like those of a boxer on the ropes and he lashed the ground with his stockwhip. The herd diverted away from them. Terry ran quickly to calm Michael's horse. He grabbed it by the reins and controlled it soothingly stroking its head.

'Are you alright Mick?' he asked.

Michael was perspiring like a waterfall and shaking nervously. 'Yeah,' he gasped. 'Thanks a lot, Terry. I reckon I can handle anything after that.'

Terry beamed with pride. He was graceful enough to make a concession to Michael. 'If you ever come back again from England I'll ask my Dad to give you a job as a horsebreaker.'

Meanwhile Roy continued to round up the cattle. He was joined by Joe and Don who rode up alongside him. While the other drovers who had joined the drive at Culgabra the stampede was slowing down.

Many of the drovers were jumping down from their horses and facing the impact of the herd full on. Johnny, in a moment of daring spirit, ran at the herd yelling and shrieking at the top of his voice. The cattle ran around and slowly began to canter.

Standing in front of the herd all the group were reacting individually. Some of the drovers lashed their stockwhips down on the ground. Others waved their arms around. Roy was very much in charge directing the drovers to various points to control the herd.

'Stampede is nearly over,' said Johnny.

'I'm bloody proud of you Jock,' Roy said.

It was all over now. That thunderous frightening sight of stampeding cattle had been reduced to a trickle now. Terry and Michael rode towards the group of drovers. Doris and Josie had arrived back. It seemed as if everybody had come through safely. That is all except one. Michael looked very hard. He could not see him anywhere.

'Where's Freddie?' he asked with a sense of urgency.

Terry suddenly looked concerned. He looked all around. There was no sign of Freddie anywhere. He looked at Michael very worriedly and then rode off in the direction of his father. Terry dismounted from his horse and went across to Roy. Michael saw them talk to each other. The expression on Roy's face changed very quickly. He was seen to speak to Johnny. Just as suddenly, Johnny pointed to a horse wandering aimlessly on the high ground. The absence of a rider on the horse gave it an almost eerie feeling.

Michael rode in to join the rest of the group. He heard Johnny ask, 'Where the hell is Freddie?'

'That's what we're going to find out,' said Roy. 'Get on your horse, Johnny. We're going for a ride.' He turned to the other drovers. 'Hey you blokes! Keep an eye on things.' He turned to Terry. 'Stay here, son. Make sure your Mum and Doris and young Mick don't follow us.'

Roy didn't hesitate. 'Let's go, Johnny.'

The two men rode off quickly. Michael had a premonition that something terrible had happened.

They were gone for a long time. In the late afternoon Johnny plodded on horseback through the gum trees in a rocky area. He had been tracing hoof prints which led to this area. The sun was flickering between the tall trees. He moved closer and closer until he made the devastating discovery he had feared. On the ground Freddie's figure was outstretched although his face was obscured by shrubs where he had fallen. Johnny dismounted. He moved forward and almost as a sign of respect to his friend, he removed his hat and clutched it to his chest.

'Oh God – no,' he murmured in a quiet, shocked voice. He called out quickly to Roy. 'Over here. Over here, Roy. He's dead.'

'Coming, Johnny.' Roy appeared from the trees. He dismounted and came across to where Freddie lay. He knelt down. Between them they examined Freddie to see what had happened to him. 'His neck is broken. He must have been thrown from his horse when he raced off on his own.'

In the background only the sounds of cicadas and insects could be heard. The two men were speechless. They could only look at each other with sadness. Their silence and expressions spoke volumes. Finally Johnny spoke but not in his flamboyant style.

'He was a hell of a man. A real good bloke. Why did it have to end for him like this, Roy?' Johnny was heartbroken. 'He went through the Somme in the last war. He went on countless bush trails. He worked in hard, tough, stinking, humid country. And it ends like this.'

Roy tried to reassure him. 'He died at his peak, doing what he really enjoyed. I'm going to miss him. He was a good mate and a fine man. They don't make too many like him.'

'By the heavens above it seems so unfair to me,' Johnny said in a voice that showed signs of anguish. 'We're within a week of getting to Ogilvie Junction and this happens to him. He was one of those blokes everyone got along with. He always gave of his best.'

Roy stood up. Johnny rose too and looked at him realising he had paid a good tribute to his late friend. 'He always gave of his best,' repeated Roy as if he was reading the words from a book, 'A good epitaph.' He stroked his chin and thought hard for a moment. 'Johnny old mate, we're not just going to say goodbye to Freddie here and now. We'll give him a top send-off tomorrow. A service in the bush …'

Again he paused for thought. 'Do you know of a passage in the Bible we might use? Something that might sum up the spirit of the man.'

'The spirit of the man?' Johnny queried. He gave it a matter of thought. Then he decided on some words he personally cherished. *The Fruit of the Spirit*. That's a passage from Galatians.'

Roy acknowledged with a nod. 'And Johnny … '

'Yes, Roy?'

'Use that creative mind of yours. Write him a poem. Some sort of tribute.'

'By tomorrow morning?' Johnny looked concerned. 'I'll do my best.'

★★★

When Roy and Johnny returned to the herd it was obvious from their faces what had transpired. A lot of tears were shed that night. Not only by the women but some of the hardened men, too. Freddie's body was collected and bound carefully in linen and cloth from the cook's wagon.

The whole herd and drovers moved to a stream close to the waterhole. It was there that Freddie would be buried and given a church service in the bush. The night before was a sombre and sad occasion. It felt as if a hush had fallen over everyone.

It was a starlit night. The stars sparkled against a lustrous black sky. There was rising smoke from a camp fire. The cattle were by the stream having quenched their thirst although slightly restless. The horses had been roped together in a makeshift corral. Some of the drovers ate their supper in sombre mood, scraping their tin plates clean, drinking tea from tin pannikins while resting against their blanket rolls and swags. They said nothing. A good mate had gone. One of their own.

Michael had never really understood the great Australian mateship until now. Friendships were forged from adversity in crisis times of Australian history. So many periods in the country's lifespan: on the gold fields at Bendigo when the first strike was made; at Gallipoli and the Somme and Beersheba; in the treacherous Outback climate when building settlements in times of great distress when cyclone, bushfire or flood struck and more especially, in the bush, where people pulled together in a courageous and hospitable manner unparalleled anywhere. Freddie had been part of this world and now he was being mourned.

Michael looked around at the camp. Some drovers squatted on their spurred boot heels. Don repeated his habit of rolling a cigarette, throwing it in the air and catching it in his lips. He sat with a tear-stained Doris and Josie, and a sad and silent Terry. A horse rolled on its back playfully in the sand. Roy walked around the camp telling everyone about the service the next day.

On a blanket roll in an isolated corner Johnny sat writing a poem in tribute to Freddie. His eyes were red. Every now and then he would

128

look up towards the burning campfire embers. For a moment he caught Michael's eye and noticed him watching. He moved his lips as if to force a smile then he continued to write. A shadow fell across him. Johnny looked up into the face of Joe.

'Boss say that Freddie's gone.'

Joe looked into Johnny's bloodshot eyes. 'Yes, he's gone,' Johnny replied in a quiet voice that almost choked with emotion and then he added, 'He's gone to the dreamtime world Joe.'

The dreamtime, a place beyond this world the Aborigines believed in. Surely Freddie would be there.

'I liked Freddie. He was a good man,' said Joe. He turned around and walked away. Johnny continued to write. On that grizzled Scotsman's face, which normally never showed a trace of emotion, Michael saw a tear form in the corner of his eye and roll down his cheek. He could have cried himself at the sight of it. Johnny's sadness was more than he could bear.

Seventeen

Close to the drovers' camp there was a small hill. A wooden cross signified Freddie Bannan's final resting place. Everyone was gathered for the service and, as a mark of respect, all the drovers removed their hats which they held to their chests. Roy had disciplined the group to ensure a sensational send-off for Freddie. The horses were all lined up in a row. The cattle were peacefully grazing in the background. Roy stood in front of the group in his role as minister.

There was not one person who did not look sombre. The hymns they sang that morning had only a harmonica for accompaniment but the words seemed to flow over the bush in a spellbinding, hypnotic manner. Michael had never heard *Jerusalem'* sung so thrillingly, not even years later at the Last Night of the Proms at the Royal Albert Hall in London. The harmonica player did not know the tune of *The Old Rugged Cross* but they sang it anyway without any musical accompaniment. In the bush setting and atmosphere the sound was quite stunning. The mixture of voices took on a rich timbre as they sang and everyone's spirits seemed to be raised. Almost in the manner of a fly-past, some brightly coloured birds flew up above the wide, blue sky.

It was certainly a service to be remembered. Josie remembered Freddie with much affection, her eyes brimmed on the point of tears but she was strong and held her emotions intact. Johnny, a man of hard appearance, felt the loss of his good friend enormously and he looked towards Freddie's grave. Somehow he found the strength within to sing to the heavens.

Terry swallowed. The occasion had brought a lump to his throat. Doris tried to keep herself erect. Michael and his Aunt Doris had both shared the same tragedy of his father Frank's death. She was still trying to come to terms with Jack's absence. He was a prisoner-of-war somewhere. That was almost certainly the case now.

It was such a poignant scene. Like a photograph years later Michael could still reproduce the image in his mind: stubble-bearded drovers; a cattle herd; horses in line; a bush setting; a cross on the hill. It was a striking scene.

At the conclusion of the hymns there was a breathtaking silence and Roy stepped forward to speak about Freddie. He delivered his words in an emotionally-charged voice that was full of strong emphasis, conviction and the sincerity he always projected.

'The outback of Australia,' Roy began, 'Is a frightening place to those who don't know it and who come here from the relative security of the big city. It is a place of hot, big distances, a red hot wilderness of few people, plants and trees that don't grow anywhere else in the world, rocks and ranges that glow iridescent in the night, animals and insects that are unique in their form. It is a place where water is scarce and the overland tracks take a lot of conquering. When city people think of the bush there's a tendency for them to think of the more famous men. Men such as the explorers: Wentworth, Blaxland, Burke and Wills; the cattle king Sidney Kidman, the Reverend John Flynn who founded the Royal Flying Doctor Service. It's the ordinary blokes they forget. Special blokes. The ones that ride the boundaries and drive the cattle for the beef they eat down there in Sydney and Melbourne. The people who shear the sheep and mind the stock. I want to pay tribute to the working man in the bush whose name doesn't become immortal or legendary. He's the man with the swag and blanket roll who comes here and builds a life for himself in conditions that would deter many a toughened man. People whose names you would forget unless they were mates of yours and mine. Mates like Freddie Bannan.' He cast a glance to Freddie's grave. Roy continued to speak, the motion surging through him. 'Yes, we lost a good mate yesterday. One of the very best. A fun-loving, humorous, hard-working larrikin who wouldn't want to be remembered any other way. He was one of those men – the characters, the working man who helped pioneer the bush along with all those drovers, stockmen, jackaroos, boundary riders and other men and women of assorted trades and professions, who came here and made it their way of life. I thought about Freddie a lot last night. The moments of friendship I shared with him. And there was much to remember. Times spent on the trail. Over a campfire when we'd sip a mug of tea and as the flames flickered late into the night, through the crackling ashes and bush smoke he would recount stories of his childhood in Adelaide; a happy one by all accounts. He would speak of his time spent in a big city bank yearning for a wider world of adventure and excitement. And, by golly, he found it, didn't he? When he was a young fellow, he roamed the bush. From Adelaide to Darwin, Coolgardie to Tibooburra. He saw it all. He came to Endeavour Downs and was one of the most enthusiastic workers we ever had. He always gave of his best.' He looked towards Johnny quickly who smiled briefly at the acknowledgement. 'In the last war he joined up uncomplainingly. He did his duty in the Dardanelles and the Somme, and when he was on leave in England before coming home he told every Pommie within earshot that Australia was the best bloody country in the world. In the years that passed I saw Freddie at work in the shearing shed. I saw him round up cattle and ride the trail. I'm going to miss him: his friendship; his loyalty; his endeavour. We're all going to miss him.' He stopped for a moment and cast his eyes to Johnny who stepped forward from the group. 'Johnny is now going to read a passage from the Bible that somehow contains qualities we might all strive to emulate. Qualities that Freddie had in abundance.'

Johnny cleared his throat and spoke the beautiful words. '*From Galatians 5: 22, 23. The fruit of the spirit is love, joy, peace, patience, kindness, goodness, faithfulness, gentleness, and self-control.*'

Just as quickly Johnny stepped back. There was a short silence as the drovers absorbed the words.

Roy continued. 'We have one final note of dedication for Freddie. Johnny has written a poem as part of our tribute today. When the poem is over we will, as a sign of respect, give two minutes 'silence in memory of Freddie, then his closest friends will scatter earth upon his grave. Immediately after we will head for our horses and we'll take the cattle on to Charleville with enthusiasm. We will finish what we started in honour of our friend, Freddie.' He smiled at Johnny. 'Read the poem, Jock. Our friend. Our mate, which is dedicated to Freddie Bannan.'

Johnny moved forward and stood slightly in front of Roy. For Johnny it was a highly emotional moment. He read from several sheets of paper occasionally glancing at the faces of the drovers before him. He was expressive and managed to read the lines in a direct and sincere manner touching the hearts of all

He was a fine man and a stout hearted bloke,

A good friend, a great listener, who'd tell you a joke.

He may even have given you a song, a funny limerick or an amusing rhyme,

And when you were face down on the floor,

He'd tell you to survive the count and get up and go back for more.

He was the friend with warm words that would reassure,

But he'd not hesitate to scorn if it was time and sympathy an idle person was stalling for,

I've met him in many a place and enjoyed the rick roistering happy moments that his company would bring,

Talk of days gone by, old friends and relatives, good humour and the tunes he and his friends would sing.

He's help the little man that life had hit hard in the side,

Yet he'd help the big man who had suffered a tumble, and emerged much more humble,

Without pride.

You probably met him many a time,

This man who was a very good friend of mine.

I'm speaking of our friend Freddie.

He was an ordinary decent bloke, not a saint, with a heart of gold who'd help a lonely person or a saddened heart,

A person who became a mate at first meeting, to whom friendship, conversation and bush folklore became an art.

The world's a better place for his old-fashioned values, decency, humour and that old-fashioned courtesy to be kind,

I expect you met people like this many a time,

And in periods of loneliness, broken hearted or dispirited and knowing so many sad hours,

The cheer and humour that this good bloke and mate could bring made one feel, "Isn't it glad that he was a very good friend of ours?"

Freddie's gone from our midst but you'll never be forgotten by any of us dear friend,

For as long as we have memories we'll remember your friendship and decency to the very end.

Valé, Freddie Bannan, Valé.'

Two minutes' silence followed Johnny's recitation. Everyone was totally absorbed in the atmosphere of the moment. There was not a murmur, a whisper or a cough to break the silence. Every man, woman and youth stood erect holding their hats to their chests as a sign of respect. Michael moved his eyes from left to right taking in all of the sight. He looked straight ahead at Roy who was standing perfectly still counting the seconds in his mind. The two minutes' silence in the early morning heat came to an end. Roy put his hat on and everyone responded by doing the same.

Roy walked across to Freddie's grave. He took some earth from the side of the hill and scattered it across the final resting place of Freddie Bannan. He was followed by Johnny who, after throwing earth over the grave, once again removed his hat. In a soft voice Michael heard him utter a few words.

'I hope you like the poem mate.' He put his hat on and walked to his horse.

The rest of the group, Josie, Doris, Terry, Don and Joe did the same. Roy and Johnny mounted their horses. Everyone else did the same and waited for the word to move out. For what seemed like an eternity they sat there, still, placid, poised to move away. Roy turned around to make sure that everyone was in position. Don habitually rolled his cigarette down the length of his trousers. Then he followed through with his routine of tossing it into the air and catching it in his lips. Almost at that split second the cigarette landed in Don's lips, Roy let out a cry to the drovers.

'Let's take them to Ogilvie Junction folks!'

Drovers around the herd let out shrieks and shouts. The cattle were stirred into movement. Dust rose into the air as the cattle drive moved out for the final leg of the journey. The herd began to move and all the drovers took control.

Before they left Michael felt the need to say farewell to Freddie privately. When he had ridden the boundaries with Freddie he had developed a close affinity and fondness for the man. Michael rode back towards Freddie's grave. He looked down at the cross. Poor Freddie. What a good bloke he had been to know. Michael took his stockwhip and placed it on the grave.

'Goodbye Freddie,' he said quietly. 'You'll meet my Dad now. I've got a feeling you'll both get on marvellously.'

He turned and rode off to join the rest. For the remainder of that epic cattle drive it was a very subdued journey. Although he was only sixteen he had grown and matured quickly. He had known a life up to then of poverty, sadness and excitement few boys of his age had known. He could sense the mood of the drovers. They just wanted to complete the journey in memory of Freddie. And for that matter Michael thought that this is what Freddie would have wanted.

The end of the journey was a colourful sight: the sunset shone brilliantly on the horizon; the cattle streamed forward, dark shadows in a mauve night against a blaze of red sky; drovers rode in and out of the herd like ghostly flickering figures in the night. There was a look to remember of 'we've done it!' on Roy's face when the herd of 5,000 went into Ogilvie Junction. Roy was thrilled. They had achieved almost the impossible. But that was only one test. They had another one to survive when a few of them stayed at a place out of town to relax after the end of the cattle drive. This one was completely unexpected.

At the end of the drive they decided to rest for a few days at a farmhouse in Ogilvie Junction and just enjoy some of the simple things in life like good old-fashioned home cooking and long luxurious soaks in hot baths. Michael did enjoy that short time. The room they ate in was very bare and basic apart from a few cupboards and a huge colonial copper stove at one end.

'It was nice of the owners to let us have this place to rest up for a while,' said Josie one night. 'Nothing beats a home cooked meal eh?'

'Too right,' said Roy. 'This is like real luxury to me. Cheaper than the Windsor down in Melbourne. Tucker cooked by my missus. This is what it's all about.'

Somehow Johnny could always find a way of espousing his own homespun philosophy. 'It was some achievement getting us here. Getting that mob of cattle with a bunch of make-believe drovers right across the country. A hell of an achievement, Roy. That's what life is really all about. Doing the sort of things others say you can't. The type of things that other people say are impossible.'

Roy was proud of this drive. 'Like crossing over the river to Jordan, or Muhammed moving the mountain. Not such a miracle really. We had a gutsy bunch. All of you. You Johnny, the ladies, and the boys. Thanks Terry. Thanks Mick. Thank you everyone.' He deliberated because he wanted to find adequate words to express his gratitude. 'Sometimes circumstances change an ordinary bloke from being maybe a pensive, gentle person who wouldn't normally give a quid for adventure then all of a sudden they're tested and put through the trials and tribulations of life, and they are called on to perform acts of self-sacrifice, endurance and courage they would never have dreamed of.'

'How did we bear up, Dad? Did we do alright?' Terry asked.

'Son, you and your Mum performed like troopers, and I'm proud of you both. You make me feel so damn good knowing I've got a couple of strong ones supporting me.' God bless, Roy. He did not forget Doris and Michael. He turned to them both. 'It would be uncharitable of me not to extend my pride to the three of you, Doris, Michael, Johnny. It's been a real pleasure having you with us.'

Doris was equally magnanimous. 'It was our privilege to be there with you.'

'I feel that way too,' Michael said trying hard to express his words of appreciation. 'Me and Terry – well we're only youngsters, but you treated us like the other blokes.'

It was then that Roy foisted a huge surprise on him. 'You earned your stripes.' He looked at Michael and smiled. 'Which brings me young fella to a little surprise we've got for you.'

His mind was in a quandary. Roy had completely amazed him. 'A surprise? For me?'

'Yeah. For sure. A real surprise.' Roy sat with his arms folded keeping him on the edge of his seat in expectation.

'Go on tell him, Roy,' Josie prompted. She was bubbling with happiness. 'We're all as thrilled for him as he will be. I'm so happy for you Mick.'

'What is it? Don't keep me in suspense,' Michael asked. He did not know whether to be happy or to be shocked. His expression registered a complete blank.

'Well it's like this Mick,' Roy said in a tone of voice so slow that Michael feared it would take all night before he got to the point. 'Terry, Josie and I were talking to this fellow in Ogilvie Junction who, like us, had an English evacuee lad staying with them. Apparently down in Sydney one of the radio stations is arranging a link-up in the studio with a lot of kids' relatives back there in Blighty. Anyway, I rang the studio last night and we've arranged for you to go down to Sydney with us next week.'

Michael was still mystified. It had not completely sunk in what was going to happen. 'What does this mean?' he asked bamboozled. 'Am I going to speak to my Mum back there in London?' Josie nodded with a sparkling smile. 'You're kidding?!' Michael was suddenly beaming with happiness.

'Isn't that just wonderful?' Aunt Doris asked him.

Suddenly everybody in the room was smiling. They were all as happy as Michael was and Terry slapped him on the back affectionately.

That same night there was an unexpected downfall of rain. Michael lay in his bunk listening to its heavy cascade on the roof. It was the type of rain he had never seen before. In Queensland, a tropical state, he knew the rainfall could be exceptionally heavy but he was surprised by the extent of this. Across the room in the half light and half shadows he could see Johnny, with whom he was sharing a room, looking out.

'Are you alright, Johnny?'

He turned to face him. 'Will you listen to that rain, Mick? It is absolutely bucketing down. It almost strikes a note of nostalgia with me. Do you know why?' Michael nodded that he didn't. He was bemused but always intrigued by Johnny's lyrical soul. 'That sound. That type of heavy rainfall is what I heard so often when I was a youngster at sea. Strange how the sounds of things can bring back a memory of one's youth.' Even stranger, thought Michael, how Johnny could speak so eloquently in long descriptive narratives. 'By God, I did know some stormy nights in the last war. At Jutland. Up and down the North Sea. I remember one lad. He was a naval rating. Same age as you. Sixteen, I tell you Michael!' He was suddenly remembering an incident in his life with passion. 'This poor, brave lad remained at his post by the big guns on deck as we were being shelled left, right and all ways. Courageous young lad. I looked away for one moment. When I looked back half the deck had been blown away and the young lad had gone.'

Michael was amazed. 'And the rainfall brought those memories back to you?' he gasped incredulously.

'Don't you ever get reminded of things, young man? You may only be sixteen but you've packed a lot in. I've not heard you talk about your Mum or Dad. You must think of them surely?'

'I do. It hurts me to think of my Dad. He was such a decent bloke. Friendly and cheerful like Freddie was.' Johnny looked at Michael with sympathetic eyes. 'You would have liked him. It upsets me when I think of nice people dying when they've got so much to give.'

Johnny showed a lot of understanding and sympathy. 'Life is like that,' he said solemnly. Then his eyes sparkled for a moment. 'Anyway, you'll be speaking to your own mother soon. Your family is the most valued thing in life, above and beyond anything else.' The rain seemed to be getting heavier and heavier. 'By God, Michael, we'll not be getting much sleep with the rainfall the way it is!'

He was curious about Johnny's past life. With the rain beating down on the roof it was obvious that sleep was out of the question for a while. He rose from his bunk.

'Do you miss Scotland, Johnny?' Michael asked. 'Got any relatives back there?'

He smiled, although he thought it was the memory of the place and not Michael's naïve question that brought this on. 'I've got an elder sister living with her family in the Borders. My own parents died when I was young. As to missing Scotland, well I've been away more than a wee while. Almost twenty five years now. Although the further away it gets the more I think of it.'

'That's a long time. I suppose you don't remember it so well?' Michael mused.

Johnny lit a gas light that flickered in the dark. His soulful face reflected over the past. 'That's just it, I remember it so well! I know the years away have changed me, and forgive me if I sound so lyrical – that's the Celt in me, but now at my age I've opinions and conviction ingrained into my character that I never knew I could possess. I'm a changed man. True. But, yet, I miss Scotland. My childhood and youth is a time I recall with a mixture of nostalgia and emotion. Time and time I have returned to it in spirit. In the years I've been away chapters of history have closed and opened with great rapidity. There has been a cavalcade of Prime Ministers in Britain.' Johnny surprised Michael by quoting the name of every one. 'Lloyd George, Bonar Law, Stanley Baldwin, Ramsay McDonald, Neville Chamberlain and Winston Churchill. The monarchs too have changed. King George V died and Edward VIII became ruler, although only for a short time until he abdicated in order to marry the woman he loved so much, he felt obliged to give up the throne for, and now we have a gentle shy man in King George VI who I think is a man worthy of great respect for the way in which he has tackled his royal duties. A role that he was unprepared for and has handled with dignity. I am perhaps rather biased for he married a fine Scottish lassie, Elizabeth Bowes-Lyon. Apart from this change of personalities in high places that the colonies reported word for word, the events I have missed include the General Strike and the Great Depression. Of course I was not immune to its worldwide effects for it too reached out here in Australia. And then of course the dark forces have given fear to many that we may become embroiled in a conflict as fierce and as devastating as the last one.'

Johnny had spoken in such an entertaining and lyrical manner that

Michael did not want to interrupt him. This rugged Scotsman was probably one of the most fascinating speakers he had ever met. It was no wonder that he, Freddie, Jack and Roy had been such a closely knit team. The pair of them stood listening to the devastating rains for a few minutes. It was beginning to sound danger. Outside it was becoming increasingly muddier. The water was flowing like a river. The downpour became steadily heavier.

'What keeps you going? Where I come from it seems to be the family.' Michael was interested in what prompted Johnny. 'People like you – and Freddie – you all seem so ...'

'Solitary?' Johnny found the word as if he was one step ahead of Michael's thoughts. 'I suppose it's my way of life. I always thought of myself as one of the last maritime adventurers and seadogs this century. A bit of a boy. A wanderer. I've lived not for security or material gain, but for the joy and the sheer thrill of life itself. I've always had my faith and trust in the Almighty and the belief in *Galatians 5:22, 23 – the fruit of the spirit of love, joy, peace, patience, kindness, goodness, faithfulness, gentleness, self-control.* It has remained my sustaining influence throughout the stormy seas I have sailed upon and my encounters with typhoon, cyclone, gale-force winds and the rough passage of life itself.' Johnny's eyes suddenly froze at the sight outside. 'Good grief!' His voice was stony cold. 'Michael I think we...'

Before he could finish what he was saying the door flew open. Roy burst in furiously. 'Fellows! Get your stuff! The farmhouse is coming apart at the seams. The rain's washing the earth away beneath us.'

Johnny and Michael needed no further prompting. They grabbed their clothes. 'The heavens are bursting surely!' he exclaimed.

'More like the floodwaters from Alvira Creek! Let's get the bloody hell out of here,' Roy retorted.

Within minutes the small group left the farmhouse. The waters were flooding down like a river. They waded through to a huge, white gum tree which was bending with the pressure forced on it by the flood waters. Each of them scrambled desperately up a tree which they hoped would be their saviour.

The rain pelted down as they tried to position themselves on the branches of the tree. Their hands and clothes were so wet and slithery they could hardly get a grip. Beneath them the farmhouse began to break up. The walls gave way with a splintering, crackling sound. The roof split in two and caved in hitting the water like falling debris. In a series of crashes the separate parts of the farmhouse fell into the water and started to drift away. Pieces of furniture drifted past. Bits of wood flowed with the water. The rain poured and poured and poured.

The entire group hung tightly to the tree. It was agony trying to hang on with all the awesome forces of nature being hurled at them. Michael's face stung from the piercing rain and wind. He closed his eyes with the sound and the fury raging all around. He opened them again at the split second that the branch Terry was sitting on began to crack at the stem. Terry was thrown off balance and lost his grip. He plunged into the waters below. Michael did not even think about what he was going to do. He responded immediately and leapt down from the tree.

It was a case of momentary madness on his part. Luckily the current swept Terry towards the tree rather than away from it. But the gushing water was too strong for both of them. They bobbed up and down in the water. Michael grabbed the truck on the tree and with his other hand stretched out to Terry who took hold of it. This caused a chain reaction of people movement. Roy slithered down a couple of branches and put his hand out to Michael. He loosened his grip around the tree and took Roy's hand. Above, Johnny was holding Roy tightly to the tree. It was one almighty fight, a tumultuous battle royal against the elements. Michael pulled Terry close. Roy pulled Michael. One by one they scrambled to a safe position up the gum tree. How it stayed there rooted deeply he did not know. That tree, however, was a safe haven. From the security it offered, the group gazed down puffing exhaustedly.

'Thanks mate. You're a good 'un,' gasped a very relieved Terry.

'I'll second that,' said Roy.

'Thank God we're all together,' Josie remarked.

Michael didn't swell with pride at his momentary act of bravado. All he could do was grimace, squeeze his sponge-wet clothes, sweep his sodden hair back over his head and wish to God that he was at home in Grenadier Guard Road.

'The horses didn't stand a chance. Got swept away,' Terry said grimly. They were beautiful horses too who had served them well all the way from New South Wales to Queensland. Michael hoped they would not suffer and would be swept on to some dry ground somewhere.

'Hang on tightly everybody,' Roy said firmly. 'I don't want to lose any of you. Are you right there, Doris?'

Aunt Doris pushed her wet hair back. 'Just, Roy, just,' she replied in a faint voice.

'What about you Jock?' Roy called out.

Johnny managed some dry humour. 'Soaking wet! Exhausted, aching all over. And one day we'll laugh about this.'

'You reckon?' Roy responded in a laconic manner.

Even in the midst of all this rain and with floodwaters surging all around Roy could laugh. 'Tell you what, folks. There must be better ways of spending an evening!'

It rained solidly all night long. Not until the middle of the next morning did it finally dissipate. Michael was starving. His stomach felt like a hollow, empty drum. He looked up at the sky and then pulled at his sodden shirt. He pinched his trousers which were also soaked. Before them lay the unbelievable sight of water flooding the plains and trees partly submerged. The sun was beginning to shine. It was silent apart from the sound of water streaming past.

The others began to stir. Poor Josie was thoroughly drained of energy and she yawned with exhaustion. Aunt Doris rubbed her clothes up and down to dry herself while she sat perilously on the edge of a huge branch. Johnny ran his hand over his tired, craggy face and winked at Terry. Roy, always the leader, looked down from his position at the top of the gum tree. Somehow he managed a smile. Heaven knows why.

Roy obviously tried to inject some more humour in the predicament. He was at his most deadpan and laconic. 'It must have been one hell of a party last night,' he said without a trace of humour as pieces of the farmhouse floated around in the floodwaters. It was hard not to smile.

'I wish I'd had a pillow,' Doris joked.

'Sorry about the beds folks,' Roy jested. 'I'll have the maid change the sheets.'

The humour boosted everyone's spirits. Josie was next. 'I've slept in some rough old places before. But I've never slept with my backside wedged into a gum tree with rain falling down on my head like water from a bucket!'

'I wonder what happened to Joe and Don,' said Johnny.

Roy seemed concerned. 'Yeah, that's right. I forgot. They were going to spend a couple more days in Ogilvie Junction before joining us. I hope that they didn't get caught in the floodwaters on the way here.'

'The lads will be alright, Roy,' said Johnny. 'They're a couple of strong blokes.'

'Do you think we'll make that radio show in Sydney?' Michael asked.

Roy reassured him. 'Yeah. We'll wait 'til the water subsides a bit and move on. Be a bit muddy though. We'll have to take every step real careful.'

'How long do we wait?' asked Terry.

Johnny looked down at the waters. 'Must have been God knows how many inches of rain last night.'

'I've never seen rain like it in all my born days,' remarked Doris.

Roy was a patient, if cautious man. 'We wait. It's as simple as that. A lot of hours yet. Treat it as thinking time. But we're not moving off yet. I'm not putting any of our lives at risk.'

It was a wise decision. The waters did not subside. The small group waited for hours and hours in the tree. Night came and they were all strained and tired. It was still and utterly quiet. Each one of them was far too exhausted now to speak. Doris appeared close to collapsing. She was struggling to keep her eyes open. For a moment she came close to losing her balance then she regained her hold.

In the distance a sound became obvious. It was only very faint. But it reminded Michael of the sound he made when he rowed his Mum and Dad down the river at Maidstone. It was a dip and splash occurring at frequent intervals in an almost rhythmic tone.

Doris leaned across to Josie. 'Can you hear that?'

'What am I listening to?' Josie strained her ears hard.

'Shhh. Listen.'

'I can hear it too,' said Michael.

The slow dip and splash continued. In the dark a swinging lantern could be seen. Just barely visible was the outline of a small rowing boat and two shadowy figures only apparent by their hats. Gradually the boat came closer and closer.

'Where should the house be Don?' A voice in the dark spoke. It was immediately recognisable as Joe.

Another voice in the dark responded. 'According to the map it should be round about where we are now I reckon. But there's nothing. The place must have been clean washed away.'

Everyone recognised their voices. There were smiles all round.

'It's the boys,' Roy said in a quiet voice full of relief. 'Don and Joe would you credit it! They must have come from Ogilvie Junction to look for us. God bless them.'

Johnny yelled out loudly. 'We're over here boys. Stuck up a gum tree!'

Down below the lantern was suddenly flickered upwards. Joe's smiling face could be seen. It was one of the most wonderful sights Michael had ever seen, he thought. Don looked up from behind at them. He smiled first then as the lantern showed them at different points on the gum tree he gaped in absolute astonishment.

'Geez, what are you'se all doing up there?' he drawled in the slow voice of a country bumpkin.

Josie exploded in laughter. 'We thought it was a good place to hold a party! What do you think we're doing up here? The farmhouse broke up in the storm.'

Don and Joe had come well prepared. Not only had they come in a boat of their own but they had another small rowing vessel attached by ropes to theirs.

'Did you fellows come looking for us?' Roy shouted down.

'Sure did,' said Joe. 'We knew you'd come up here to get a bit of peace.'

Don called back. 'We've got this boat attached to ours. You can split up amongst the two boats if you like. Feel free to join us if you're not doing anything.'

Roy smiled. 'You blokes stay right there! We're coming down.'

Don and Joe swung the two boats over to the bottom of the gum tree. Very soon, the bedraggled figures descended gratefully into the boats. When everyone was in place the boats moved off in the general direction of Ogilvie Junction from when they would soon depart for Sydney.

Eighteen

After that exciting episode of Michael's life he was pleased to head back to some civilised life in the city for a couple of weeks. When one says civilised, it depends on how a particular person views that word. It was civilised in the city in terms of accommodation, trams, hot and cold running water and a comfortable lifestyle. Years later looking back Michael thought the bush and the people who lived there were more civilised and compassionate than any other place he lived in.

Sydney in 1944 was a very different city from the fine metropolis it is today. Its magical centrepiece in those days was the Sydney Harbour Bridge before being partly eclipsed in later years by the sparkling white sails of the Opera House at Bennelong Point. It was hard not to fall in love with this city. Michael had only seen it briefly when he had arrived. Now he was seeing it in full detail.

They stayed at a bed and breakfast hotel in Darlinghurst Road in the raffish suburb of Kings Cross. All the obvious signs of wartime were there. Soldiers and sailors from the Pacific Fleet thronged the streets and thoroughfares. The women of Sydney looked stunningly beautiful. They still do. Yet despite the war the people seemed to be enjoying themselves. They rode on the tram to Bondi Beach, crossed the harbour to Manly on the ferry and generally enjoyed this rare taste of big city life.

But they did not forget the real purpose of the journey to Sydney. On a fine night Roy, Josie, Doris, Johnny, Terry and Michael made their way to a radio station where the international link-up was to take place. Michael could not say he wasn't excited. He truly was. He also felt nervous and on edge.

Inside the vast auditorium of the radio station, which belonged to the Australian Broadcasting Commission, the interior was packed full of people. An announcer with a voice like honey and manners as smooth as silk guided children up from the audience to speak to their relatives far away. Down in among a very tearful audience Michael sat anxiously waiting for his turn to go up to the microphone.

It had been four years since he had last spoken to his dear old Mum back there in bombed-out London. He sat there watching the other youngsters going up to the microphone and speaking to their mums and dads in England. Michael was beginning to shake inside. He was on edge with excitement. It was an emotional evening for so many of the youngsters who had been evacuated to Australia during the war.

Finally, the announcer on stage started the introduction for Michael, who began to quiver inside. He felt as if he was about to turn into a mass of jelly. How could he possibly be so nervous? He had been sent to Australia on a remote cattle station in the middle of the Outback. He had been on a cattle drive. He had survived a torrential flood. How could he be nervous?

Michael could feel Aunt Doris's hand on his shoulder firming him up. The announcer spoke in a gentle tone. Michael steadied himself. One thing worried him. How did he speak to his Mum and acknowledge what had happened to his Dad? Before he could think about that any more the announcer began to say the important words which would indicate for Michael to walk up to the stage and join him.

'Now, ladies and gentlemen, for our next reunion over the air on the ABC Network we turn to a young lad from London. We've had evacuees speak to their families in the English counties of Surrey, Yorkshire, Kent and Sussex. Now we're going to reunite an English Cockney lad, a true Londoner born within the sound of Bow Bells, with his mother over the airwaves. He's here tonight with his Aunt Doris. He comes from Grenadier Guard Road in the East End of London.' The announcer looked down at the audience. 'Are you there Michael Forbes?'

Michael stood up and felt Aunt Doris thrust him forward. The others in their bush ways immediately gave him a cheer and a round of applause. This prompted the whole audience to join in. Michael was slightly embarrassed although glad to see that his friends from Endeavour Downs Station did not stand on ceremony. He walked down the aisle way putting on a happy smile. Suddenly he felt marvellous. The announcer was as happy as he was and shook Michael's hand when up came on stage.

'Michael Forbes. Ladies and gentlemen, give him a hand!' The audience applauded once more. 'Welcome young man. How do you feel?'

'A little bit nervous I guess.'

He was extremely warm hearted. 'Well, there's no need to be, son. These might be dark days of war but in here you're among friends.' He addressed the audience now. 'Let me tell you a little bit about Michael everyone. He was brought up by his Mum and Dad, Honeysuckle and Frank Forbes, in London's East End. His Dad, Frank, sadly is no longer with us, but his Mum is sitting there in London with some family friends of yours, the Corrigans, Spangler and Cherry.' This immediately brought a smile to Michael's face at the thought of this lovable pair being there with his Mum. The announcer went on to describe Michael's recent history to the audience. 'When the war came Michael was evacuated out here to stay with his Aunt Doris at Endeavour Downs Station.' He turned to face him. 'I believe you've had quite a bit of excitement recently Michael?'

'I've just come back from a cattle drive,' he replied. 'With a few of my friends there we went across to Ogilvie Junction in Southern Queensland.'

'From Endeavour Downs?' the announcer inquired with genuine interest. 'That is some trek.' He reverted to the matter in hand. 'Well for a young man of your age you've packed a lot in. Your Mum would be certainly proud of you,' he added. 'And I'm happy to know she is. Just step over here to this microphone.' They moved a couple of places to another microphone. Michael could feel the tension surging through him. The announcer spoke into the microphone. 'Mrs Honeysuckle Forbes of Grenadier Guard Road, London, how are you today?'

It was all too much for Aunt Doris in the audience. Her eyes brimmed with tears. She reached for her handkerchief.

From within the microphone Honeysuckle's voice came across loud and clear. 'I'm fine, thank you, sir.'

The announcer was gentle and sensitive. 'You're going to feel even better in a minute.' He turned to Michael and spoke softly. 'Michael it's been four – nearly five years. Say hello to your mother, son.'

The audience was hushed. Doris was streaming tears. Johnny's eyes were moist. Josie was beginning to show signs of tears. Roy smiled at the poignancy of the moment. Terry watched keenly. Michael moved to the microphone. For a moment he felt apprehensive and nervous. He began to speak but his mouth dried up. He tried again.

'Hu-hullo Mum,' he splurged. He was hardly original in his choice of words.

Then Honeysuckle's voice responded in a cheerfully Cockney patter.

'Oh Mick, it's good to hear your voice. It's been so long. How are you, son? Are you well and fit? And suntanned like all the Aussies?'

Michael was shaking with emotion but his Mum's cheerful tones brought out a smile in him. 'I'm not sure about tanned. A bit blim'ing sunburnt if you ask me!' A few people in the audience laughed at this chance remark. 'It's good to speak to you, Mum.'

Honeysuckle's Cockney tones came through again. 'How are they all looking after you?'

'They've been wonderful, Mum. They have all asked me to send you their best wishes. Doris is down in the audience weeping buckets of tears. She sends her love.' He could feel his cheerfulness turning to emotion. 'I've missed you, Mum. I'm sorry about Dad. But I'll be home soon, Mum. I'll be able to give you a hand with everything.'

'Don't worry, Mick. We all got through. Mind you, Grenadier Guard Road is looking slightly different than before. People have been good. They've all been pulling hard together. Its been marvellous just how good folk have been when things have been down. Its brought out the best in us. I'm proud of you, Mick. I know it was hard for you when your Dad and I sent you out there when the war began, but you've handled it well. We're all proud of you. And I've got a couple of your old friends here who want to say hullo.'

A couple of voices came through that generated warmth. 'Hullo, me old mate! How are you Mick? It's Spangler here. Spangler Corrigan with his vivacious wife, Cherry, sitting by my side and just bursting to say hullo to the young lad Down Under.'

'Lots of love to you, darling. We're all missing you and looking forward to seeing you when this rotten old war is all over and done with. Look after yourself. God bless you. Bye now.'

Michael bid them farewell. 'Thank you Spangler. Thank you Cherry.'

Honeysuckle's voice came back. 'I thought that would surprise you. Its been so good to talk again if only for a few minutes or so. I know they wanted to say hullo. When I told some of the neighbours I was coming along to speak to you in a broadcast they had lots of questions about your life in Australia but if I asked them all I'd be here all night.'

'Let me tell them a bit, Mum.' Michael spoke with a glowing confidence he had not possessed four years before. 'Endeavour Downs is right in the bush. The nearest town is Broken Hill. Endeavour Downs has cattle, sheep, orchards of course. The place is run by Roy Lane and his wife, Josie. Their son, Terry, is about my age. We both learnt lessons over the wireless from Broken Hill although I finished by schooling really a couple of years ago. I've been doing lots of things round the station. I was a tar boy in the shearing sheds. I helped to brand the cattle. I did some jackarooing. I rode the boundaries fixing fences. I did a bit of carpentry work with Johnny McCullough – he's the resident carpenter. He's a Scot from Glasgow originally. Then we've just finished a cattle drive across to Queensland. I've done so much, Mum. I can't believe it. Do you think that answers all their questions?'

From England his mother replied. 'It certainly does love!'

'Tell me a bit more about what you're doing Mum,' Michael asked. He was worried that the conversation was becoming a little one-sided. 'I read your letters but you never tell me too much.'

'Well since your Dad …' Mum hesitated and rephrased her words. 'As you know, Spangler and Cherry have been with me. We've all been looking after each other. I've been working down at one of the factories during the day and in the evening I've been helping out at a local rest and recreation centre for servicemen and women.'

At this point the announcer moved up behind Michael. He spoke into the microphone during a pause. 'Honeysuckle it's been wonderful to reconcile you and your son, Michael, over the thousands of miles that separate our two countries. You'll appreciate we have other families we want to reunite over the airwaves which just leaves us a few moments for last minute messages. Honeysuckle, do you have a final message for Michael here?'

'I do, sir,' she replied. 'Michael?'

'I'm still here, Mum,' he answered.

Her voice came across in a tone of finality although the old Cockney warmth bubbled in every syllable. 'Take care, son. I love you. Look after yourself. God willing, we'll all be reunited soon.'

'And you, Mum. Love you too,' Michael said feeling a little shaky.

The announcer took over. He was diplomatic and skilled with words. 'Honeysuckle and Michael, thank you for appearing in the broadcast. I know its been an emotional experience for all of us here and we are sincere when we say that our prayers are with you over there in the old country particularly for you and your people in the East End of London who went through the ordeal of the Blitz. We wish you well and thank you again for your participation.'

Honeysuckle was not to be outdone. She had one final thing to say. 'Thank you again sir, I'm sure a lot of people here wish all the Aussies the very best too. I would like to thank all of those good people who have looked after my son. Good wishes to Australia.'

The announcer responded. 'Thank you, Mrs Honeysuckle Forbes in London!' The audience loudly applauded. This very courteous man turned to Michael and shook his hand. 'Thank you, Michael Forbes.' He showed him the way down the auditorium to rejoin the others. When Michael got back to his chair Roy ruffled his hair and grinned warmly. The others looked moist-eyed yet the warmth of their characters was firmly evident in the happiness they felt for him.

The next day they all left Central Station on a train bound for Endeavour Downs. In his mind he had the thought that perhaps the years out in Australia were drawing to a close. Michael was right. Just over a year later the war in Europe would end.

Nineteen

One glorious day in 1945 there were celebrations all over the world. Victory in Europe – VE Day. That was what the headlines screamed out.

Crowds filled the streets in faraway London to celebrate. From the balcony of Buckingham Palace, Winston Churchill and the Royal Family waved to the people below. Peace at last. People danced in Leicester Square and Piccadilly. There were tears and laughter, kisses and hugs. New songs to be sung. Perhaps you were there?

In America they went wild. Well the Yanks like a good party, don't they? And hell they had a wild rip-roaring time in New York. They celebrated in a blizzard of ticker tape and goodwill. Right along Fifth Avenue they danced. In Times Square they sang. They did the conga in Madison Avenue.

All over Australia people celebrated. At Endeavour Downs cattle station they cheered as they listened to the wireless. An announcer called Talbot Duckmanton of the Australian Broadcasting Commission described the scene of crowds in Martin Place, Sydney.

On VJ Day in August 1945 there was a man called Ern Hill who was so happy he almost flew into the air as he danced with joy among the crowds in Sydney's Castlereagh Street. The image of the 'dancing man' symbolised the great joy that gripped Australia on that memorable day and that newsreel picture is still played today in some documentaries.

Back at Endeavour Downs Station Roy Lane had one of the biggest celebrations ever held west of Broken Hill. Josie played the piano happily. Roy, Johnny and Doris were in the highest of spirits. Terry and Michael joined in the fun and sang along. After five years Michael could sign the old Australian songs with the best of them. Did they sing that night! Did they ever! Friends and neighbours from nearby farms came to join them. Don and Joe smoked cigars. A lot of beer filled a lot of glasses. They sang 'Waltzing Matilda' and the 'Road to Gundagai' and 'Five Miles to Gundagai' and *'Suvla Bay'*. They stood on tables and sang *'Advance Australia Fair'*. Never had an anthem been sung so proudly that day.

That night really brought home the truth to Michael. The European War was over. It was only a matter of time before he would soon be going home: to London. A different London now: Burned out, tired and blitzed. Yet he would be going home, eager, enthusiastic and with maturity beyond his years perhaps, although that was something he would leave to others to judge.

Michael would be going back to his Mum and all the faces of the past: Spangler, Cherry, May and Dolly who he felt sure would return just to swab that front step and old Bert Greaves, the happy policeman. Would they all be there? He looked across to his Aunt Doris. He thought that he would be going home alone. He did not know then that his Aunt Doris would be travelling with him.

Uncle Jack did not return home from the war. There's a place somewhere in the Far East when the sun glitters brightly through swaying palm trees that shroud a cemetery. Jack's buried there along with many of his comrades who died working on that notorious Burma railway. What a terrible cost of life!

During those years they had all lost someone close. But now they had the future to face. After every tragedy people face in life there is one abiding fact. They must keep going.

With the surrender of the Japanese soon after came the news about Jack. Aunt Doris who barely had two years of marriage before her husband joined up, now decided to leave as well. It was heartbreaking for her. But she too believed that life must go on. In due course she and Michael were booked to sail from Sydney.

It was a sad day of farewells when Aunt Doris and Michael left Endeavour Downs for the last time. At the front of the house some of the new station hands brought out their cases and placed them in the truck. Roy and Josie left the house first followed by Terry and Johnny. Finally, Doris and Michael walked from the house for the last time. Don and Joe stood close by. Michael watched with nostalgic thoughts as Don rolled his cigarette down the length of his trousers, tossed it into the air and caught it in his lips. He had never failed to catch it in all the time Michael had known him.

Michael shook hands with Don and Joe and Aunt Doris hugged them both. He saw a tear in Joe's eye. It felt like he was losing part of his family. Johnny got into the driver's seat. Roy and Josie sat in the front next to him. Terry held the door open while Doris entered. Terry and Michael got in and closed the doors. Johnny started up the truck. Doris had sadness in her eyes. They both turned around in their seats to take a last look at Endeavour Downs Station. 'That first golden time' Josie had spoken of when she had met Doris. Now it was all over.

Doris was looking back remembering the first time she saw it over six years before. The view had hardly changed. On the flat plateau there were the white huts and buildings, the artesian wells, some water tanks, the orchards that belonged to Jack, the sheep paddocks and riding across the horizon line were a few jackaroos. It all made for a memorable final scene.

Michael watched Doris. Her expression was at breaking point. Tears began to fall. She told him later she was remembering the first words of introduction to Endeavour Downs Station.

It was Freddie Bannan who said the opening words that lingered on in her memory. 'Endeavour Downs Station. Isn't it beaut? Big too. This is only the beginning of it'. Doris changed her expression to a gentle smile as she recalled Freddie's words.

Jack had been equally enthusiastic. 'This is it, love. This is your new home'.

Perhaps the greatest pain Doris felt was when she recalled her own words. 'This is it. Gosh I think you're right, Jack. This is going to be different for me and exciting'.

Aunt Doris was just about to wipe away a tear when Michael handed her his handkerchief. He had been watching her expression. She took the handkerchief gladly and attempted to smile through the tears. It was Michael's turn now to realise that he did not want to leave either. The vehicle sped on through the bush.

At the railway siding that passed for a railway station they stood waiting patiently. Far away a spiral of smoke filtered up into the wide deep blue Outback sky. It would only be a matter of minutes before it arrived.

'Here it comes. Right on time too.' Terry had spotted it before everybody else. Michael would miss Terry. He was now eighteen. They had become great friends during the past five years.

Josie who always sensed acutely how Doris felt turned to her. 'We're going to miss you, Doris.' After a pause she said something that probably needed to be said. 'Jack would have been proud of you.'

Doris whispered to her in confidence. 'Oh Josie. If only he'd come back from the damned war. We had so much to look forward to. So much we wanted to do.'

'I know,' said Josie sympathetically. 'But yesterday's gone, love. You've got tomorrow now. That's what counts.'

The train came closer and closer. It looked like little more than a blessed cattle truck. Michael thought with dismay of the hours ahead he would perspire in the stinking heat before arriving at Sydney's Central Station.

Roy turned to Doris and Michael. 'This is it, folks. There's a ship in Sydney waiting for you.'

'You'll write, won't you?' Josie sounded pleading. 'You won't forget us, will you? Do you hear me you two?'

Doris replied in a strong, firm voice. 'I'll never forget all of you. I promise. You've been wonderful to both of us. I'll never forget your warm welcome to me Josie. You've been a great friend to me.'

It was Michael's turn now. 'I second that. This has been something special to me.'

Josie hugged each of them. It was at that moment the train pulled into the station. Roy and Johnny picked up their cases and put them on the train.

Terry moved forward and shook Michael's hand. 'See you later, mate. You're not a bad bloke for a Pommie.'

Michael had to smile at Terry's humour. He was always the fair dinkum Aussie. 'You're not a bad bloke yourself, Tel,' he responded. 'Take it easy cobber.'

Josie hugged him again. The warmth of her smile emanating from those tired eyes and that suntanned crinkly face was far more stronger than any words. Roy shook hands with Michael in a firm no-nonsense grip.

'So long, son.' He turned to Doris and embraced her. 'You've proved yourself to be a real strong girl, luv.'

'It's been a real privilege to have known you,' said Doris.

Roy was not a man for tears or emotion. But Doris heard his voice drop an octave and slightly falter. 'You'd better get on that train otherwise we won't let you go.'

There was almost an invisible force tugging at Michael, trying to pull him back from entering the train. He didn't want to go. But he thought of home and his Mum and he reluctantly let go of the present. Johnny stood by the train door holding it open for the both of them. Aunt Doris smiled at him and she gave him a quick embrace.

'I haven't forgotten you.' Doris looked at this colourful character. 'You old rough diamond Scotsman with a sentimental heart.'

'God bless you Doris,' he said in a soulful manner.

Michael thrust his palm forward to shake Johnny's hand. 'Goodbye. Best of luck to you.'

'And you Michael. Have a safe journey home.' Johnny pinched his hat. Aunt Doris and Michael mounted the carriage and made their way to their seats. They looked through the window and waved. The train began to move. For the last time they saw Josie, Terry, Roy and Johnny together. Johnny in a last final gesture of farewell removed his bush hat and waved it. Roy pinched the rim of his hat and nodded. Josie wiped a tear away and waved. Terry smiled, removed his hat and held it to his chest.

Michael swallowed. Although he felt a deep sadness about leaving this place that had been his home for the past five years he felt excited about going home. During the night hours he thought about all the things that had happened to him since 1939. He could not see how he could ever have such greater experiences if he lived to be one hundred.

At Circular Quay in Sydney a few days later Doris and Michael boarded the liner for the six-week cruise home to England. Their years in Australia had come to an end.

Twenty

England. This is England. Michael kept saying it to himself over and over again. Six weeks later he and Aunt Doris had returned home. It was a strange feeling coming home after years away. Every sight and sound had taken on a new meaning to him. In actuality he was the Englishman coming home after a long spell abroad. But to Michael he felt more like an Australian seeing England for the first time.

When the boat had docked at Southampton Doris and Michael had taken the train to London. Outside they were passing lush green fields now. The country cottages and rectangular fields looked immensely welcoming. Michael had forgotten just how green England was. He had forgotten the marvellous sight of English trees in full bloom, people baling hay, the fruit pickers taking their produce straight from the tree and throwing it into baskets below. He looked at the flowers and fauna. There was a mild blue sky with clouds that indicated rain was round the corner.

Doris and Michael looked at the people close by in the train carriage. There was a Royal Navy sailor, men in flat caps and trilbys, businessmen in double-breasted suits, a chirpy mother with her schoolchildren. That day as they listened to the voices and the accents they realised they were well and truly home. A Cockney ticket collector in uniform spoke in sharp, cheerful tones punctuating the air with vowels each of them would have recognised in Grenadier Guard Road.

Aunt Doris seemed a long way away. She felt a sense of failure at coming home. The loss of Jack had been a devastating blow for her. In her heart she knew that for as long as she lived, there would never be another man for her. Doris was close to forty now. She was still a very eligible woman but had doubts that she would ever marry again.

Eventually the train arrived at Waterloo Station. People departed in droves from the carriages. There were soldiers, sailors, airmen, businessmen and schoolchildren all flooding the platform. Railway porters picked up baggage and parcels. Somewhere in the background a railway stationmaster called out 'Waterloo Station. All change! All change here please!' Aunt Doris and Michael picked up their cases and walked along the platform.

'I never thought I'd ever come back to London a widow,' she said in an unexpected moment of revelation.

'Don't think about it like that Aunt Doris. It's the future that counts.'

'You're right there, Mick,' she said in a positive tone.

They stopped for a moment as some porters wheeled baggage in front of them.

'I wonder where they are?' Doris had fully expected Maisy, Spangler and Cherry to be there. 'London. I can't believe we're home again, Mick.'

Almost as soon as she had spoken, a familiar voice rang in their ears from a few inches away. 'Over here, love!'

It was Honeysuckle. After five years Michael's Mum was there waiting at the platform. He ran over and hugged her. He could hardly believe it.

'Mum! Oh Mum!' he said excitedly. It was a very emotional reunion – they were both in tears. Doris ran forward and poor Honeysuckle was lost between embracing them both.

Honeysuckle's eyes flooded with tears. She had hardly changed except for a few lines but her jovial, cheerful expression and inbuilt smile was still there.

'Mick. You've grown so much,' Honeysuckle spoke in genuine surprise. 'I can't believe how much. You really are tanned like all the Aussies.' She touched Doris's arm. 'Oh it's so good to have you both home again. You'll never know how much I've missed you both.' They put their arms around each other and began to walk across the platform. 'Doris …?' Honeysuckle said abruptly. 'About Jack, I'm so sorry, love.'

'We'll pull together Honeysuckle. We've all lost someone.' Doris reassured her. 'Won't we Mick?'

'Too right we will,' he agreed. 'We're home now Mum.'

★★★

The three of them did pull together during the next year. There was never a day that Michael did not value the time spent with what little family he had left. He worked hard regrettably at a local factory although thankfully it was not the sauce factory. That factory had received a direct hit during the Blitz. Michael found work in a food factory where he worked double shifts and weekends for an entire year. There was one objective he had in mind; to move him and his mother to a place in Kent away from the memories of the past.

Within a year he had found some rented rooms in Maidstone for his mother and Doris. Michael had also found work on a farm at Yalding where he would be employed for several years. Eventually when he married and had his own family he moved to the South Coast of England to live and work in the old Roman town of Chichester in Sussex where he would spend many happy years.

In 1946 he came home from a day's hard graft to Grenadier Guard Road where a party for his nineteenth birthday had been planned. He entered the house to find himself confronted by several happy smiling faces who sang *'Happy Birthday'* to him in chorus. Aunt Doris, Honeysuckle, Spangler, Cherry and a few others such as May Maguire and Dolly Mandolino from the neighbourhood were all singing. Michael was thrilled and delighted at his surprise party.

'Happy Birthday Michael,' said Honeysuckle.

He gave her a hug. 'Thanks Mum. Thanks everyone.'

Spangler was right on form as usual. 'What about a speech then young Michael?'

'How could I refuse my honorary Uncle?' Michael said confirming the longstanding affection they had for each other. 'Well – er – alright then. Yes. A speech it is.' He hesitated as he thought of something to say. Spangler was hurriedly filling everyone's glass and handed Michael a shandy. 'Yes there is something I want to say on this, my nineteenth birthday. Its been almost a year since Aunt Doris and I returned home from Australia. I know we've all come through a lot in the past few years. I didn't imagine that when I went away as an evacuee that I would be away for all those years. And Aunt Doris never expected to come home. Both she and Jack went out to start a new life. Well the war took Uncle Jack and my Dad, Frank …' He pointed to a portrait photograph of his father on the mantelpiece. 'Anyway, we've all survived. I'm grateful to you Spangler and Cherry for looking after my Mum. Being together with you all is wonderful. Seeing everybody again is wonderful. I grew to love Australia – and Australians – while I was out there, but nothing could really take away from me the fact that this is home. This is where Mum is. The people I know. It is good to know you're all here and that despite the war, which took so many of our old friends and neighbours around here, that we are all together again to remember them with love and respect. It's good to be home. I expect Mum has told you that my late Dad – God bless his soul – had long wanted to live in Kent where we used to go hopping in the old days. Well as it were I've got myself a job down in Yalding and Mum and Aunt Doris are moving down to Maidstone. I want you to know that you'll always be welcome to come and see us whenever you want. I guess that's about it.'

'I think we ought to have a toast,' said Honeysuckle.

'I reckon you're right there Mum. To you all ...'

Spangler interrupted him sharply. 'Hold on there! It's your birthday. We should be toasting you!'

Cherry agreed. 'That's right, young man. You've grown well and it's your day today.'

Michael was equally insistent. 'No! I won't hear of it. You've all been so good to us. I would like to do the honours here. To you all, the people of my childhood and youth, this toast is for you all. Good health and happiness everlasting. Cheers Ladies and Gents.'

Honeysuckle raised her glass in the middle of the room and toasted everyone. 'To my son, Michael. Grown up to be a good bloke like his old man.'

Michael felt embarrassed because he had never thought he was anywhere near as good as his Dad. Still, it provided a glowing start to the party. Everybody started to enjoy themselves in a flurry of conversation and singing. Spangler was in his element pouring drinks and singing. People started to dance. It was a typical East End party just like the days of old before the war except everybody was older, wiser and more experienced in life now.

Later that evening Michael was to receive an even bigger surprise. While his birthday party become more fun-filled and boisterous as the hours rolled by, outside Grenadier Guard Road was deserted except for one lone shadowy figure who made his way slowly in the cold and fog. Out on the street the sound of the singing at Michael's party could be heard loud and clear. The man wore a flat cap and overcoat belted tightly in the cold night air. Finally, he arrived at the house, checked the number and knocked on the door.

Inside the house the party was going strong. Quite a few neighbours had come in for the fun. Michael was happily talking to a couple of young girls. Honeysuckle and Aunt Doris sat talking to a high spirited Spangler and Cherry.

'Was that a knock on the door?' asked Honeysuckle who was straining her ears to hear amid the din of the party.

'Sounded more like a drum roll to me,' remarked Cherry.

'I'll get it,' volunteered Doris. 'What shall I do if it's a neighbour complaining about the noise?'

Spangler as always had a suggestion. He slurred his words as he spoke. 'T-t-tell him to come in for a drink and ask – ask him to invite us to his next party at his place.'

'Sounds like good advice to me,' Honeysuckle chuckled.

Doris moved through the various people and opened the door. She was totally unprepared for who she was about to see. The first sight was of a man in a long coat and cap with his back towards her. He turned around slowly and smiled at her warmly.

'G'day, Doris. I hope I didn't shock you?'

Doris was stunned beyond disbelief. The grey hair and the lived-in face and the Scottish accent. It was all so unbelievable. 'Johnny McCullough! Johnny! Here! I don't – don't believe it! What – are you doing?' She stopped in mid-sentence and hugged him. 'How wonderful to see you. Come on in.'

'It's great to be here Doris,' he said. 'I'm on my way home to Scotland.' Doris almost pulled him into the room. She was so thrilled to see him. They entered the room and most people just regarded him as another person who had dropped by for the party. Doris suddenly clapped her hands and made an announcement to the party. Michael looked up and could not believe his eyes. There across the room was somebody from Endeavour Downs Station in the Outback.

'Johnny!' Michael gasped in utter amazement.

'Can I have your attention everyone?' Doris demanded. 'This fine fellow here is Johnny McCullough, a good friend of ours from Australia. Would you all make him feel most welcome!'

Spangler was the first on his feet. 'Be glad to.' He shook Johnny's hand setting the precedent and others followed.

Michael made his way across to see him. 'Good to see you again Michael,' said Johnny.

'I would never have believed it.' It was so unexpected to see this craggy old fellow again. 'Johnny McCullough,' Michael repeated still surprised beyond description. 'All the way from Australia!'

Much later in the early morning hours when the partygoers had left and Honeysuckle had sleepily retired to her bed Johnny talked of his most recent experiences. Michael listened avidly with Doris. Johnny still spoke in his romantically descriptive manner. Michael and Doris were the captive audience eager to listen to Johnny's nostalgic tones.

'Well the party's over,' said Doris pouring tea for the three of them. 'Everyone's gone home. Honeysuckle's gone to bed. Spangler and Cherry have gone to bed too. Don't worry about going back to your hotel, Johnny. You're welcome to stay here the night.'

Johnny sipped his tea and nodded. 'Thank you, Doris. I'll be taking my leave of you first thing in the morning. I have to catch the train to Glasgow mid-morning.'

'I'm still amazed to see you here,' said Michael. 'What brings you home after all these years?'

'Yes, indeed,' said Doris also curious about Johnny's presence here. 'It's been a fair few years since your boots touched British soil.'

Johnny realised he had a keen audience and eased himself into the focal point. Although he phrased his words poetically and was long on description there was never any doubt that he was a most sincere man, yet entertaining with his powers of eloquent expression.

'Why did I come home?' Johnny spoke as if he was asking Doris and Michael. 'To be honest and direct with you Doris, I would have to say that it was a case of rediscovering my roots. I mean, I've been a roaming bachelor with no marital or romantic ties, apart from – if you'll excuse the somewhat candid admission – the occasional discretion or dalliance over the years – and I'm a man in my fifties, with no permanent home, just a few obscure relatives north of the border, and a longing for something stable, secure and offering comfort. For the best part of twenty-seven years I've lived in tropical climates. Now as the evening shadows of my lifetime fall I have that desire to experience once again the feel of the hills, the gorse and the heather, the spring water freshness, and to walk across dales where, when the wind blows, you feel in its cold gusts the hint of polar ice and up in the Northern skies the Aurora Borealis looms bright and flickering. You must excuse me for my rambling talk.'

'No. Do go on Johnny,' Doris insisted. 'Hearing you speak again is reminiscent of those campfire stories and poems we heard on the bush trail to Queensland.'

Johnny sipped his tea and smiled at the memory of it. He was completely relaxed. 'I'm beginning to feel a bit like Long John Silver coming home to the Admiral Benbow Inn to recount his years of swashbuckling and plundering! Philandering – yes! Plundering – no! I've never had the opportunity.' This remark raised a smile with Doris and Michael. 'No, when I get home I'll not be spinning yarns over an ale in a corner pub. I'd be telling true tales that no accomplished liar or weaver of legends could ever match.'

'You must have been sad to leave?' Michael asked.

'Perhaps I was initially,' Johnny replied. 'But when I boarded the flying boat at Rose Bay in Sydney, in anticipation of a trip that was to take me a little over a week and across many lands, suddenly it became the most joyous feeling I had known when I began my long journey home. When the vessel skimmed across the shimmering blue waters of the harbour and I gazed for the last time at the great steel bridge affectionately known as the 'coathanger' that spans the two sides of Sydney together, I have to admit that I felt a momentary sadness at leaving such a beautiful city. But that was soon dispelled as I thrilled to the feel of my first flight and the powerful roar of the engines as we became airborne. I will always remember that epic flight and the places we stopped at and flew over. Travelling with the same group of people for about a week I got to know my companions and crew quite well even though their personalities and professions were, in contrast to my humble work, quite different.'

Doris was quick to assure him. 'You underestimate yourself, Johnny. I think you would fit in well anywhere you go. There's no doubt you're a good solid working man but I feel you could hold your own in any company.'

'I try to. I've long had a distaste of distinctions in class and rank,' he answered, never lost for words.

'Where did the flying boat travel to, Johnny?' Michael asked him.

Johnny answered in a description that was more interesting than any geography lesson Michael had ever been taught at school. 'Leaving the harbourside of Sydney we flew across some rugged land touching down briefly at a salt lake in South Australia. It's amazing you know looking down at the vast expanse of the bush that stretched below. Air flight gives one a clear picture of the size and nature of this land. Australia yielded sizeable cattle stations and settlements that are far flung and mere blots on a map of this parched continent.'

'Don't we know that?' Michael agreed. 'Endeavour Downs was one of those blots.'

'That's for sure,' Doris said thinking back to that first golden time.

Johnny continued. 'Anyway we flew on to the steaming tropical heat of Darwin in the Northern Territory for an overnight stay. From Darwin we flew across to Indonesia where we stopped at places with curious names such as Dili, Duteng and Bandung. At Bandung in the most tepid, sticky heat while the aircraft was being refuelled, the passengers and crew were served a meal in a tent on a makeshift airstrip. Every few minutes or so the tablecloth was removed thick with insects clogging the material and a new one was placed down. Close by dark-skinned waiters rushed around at great pace in the uncomfortable humidity, trying very hard to please their guests in every way. We flew on to Singapore, Kota Bharu and Rangoon; always flying low over jungles, mountain scenery, temples, pagodas, villages and landscapes of varying colours and shades. Sometimes the aircraft would glide down onto a lake or a glittering tropical sea before ascending and continuing on to its next destination.'

'And the passengers, Johnny? What were they like?' Doris enquired.

'They were a mixture. As I mentioned before, I felt humble in profession alongside of them having been mainly a manual labourer for most of my working years. However, I considered my intellect to be their equal for I have read deeply in my private hours and my personal knowledge of world events and history was as good a match for anyone's. The other passengers were mainly businessmen, government officials, several women of apparent affluence, and an English lecturer who was pleasant and charming and whose subject matter was history. In him I found a useful ally for conversation and at each major port of call, he could always tell me an historical anecdote. At Singapore he pointed out Raffles Hotel and he told me of the famous people who had stayed there such as Rudyard Kipling, and he recounted to me the tale of the time a tiger wandered into the billiard room.'

'Really!' exclaimed Doris. 'A tiger in the billiard room!'

Johnny laughed. 'I bet that gave the players more than a little cause for concern. I enjoyed his company. He was immensely entertaining and informative. He told me stories about Burma's history and the 'Road to

162

Mandalay' and he was a good travelling companion who had no reservations about class distinction or self-assured superiority because of his academic role in life.'

Michael was interested in the route that the flying boat would have taken. 'You would have flown over all the Dominions as my teacher at Britannia Street School used to refer to them.'

'The Dominions? The British Empire? Call it what you will,' said Johnny. 'All the way on that journey I was conscious of the fact that many of the ports of call were part of an empire where the sun is yet to set and the Union Jack lowered. The places we went – oh my goodness – Dacca, the Ganges delta, Delhi, Karachi, Abadan, Basra, Damascus, the Sea of Galilee, Alexandria, Crete, Venice, numerous stops across France, until finally one beautiful cool afternoon the flying boat came to rest in Poole Harbour in Dorset and I realised with sheer delight that I was home again in the British Isles after twenty-seven years away.'

'It's an awfully good feeling coming home again,' Michael said thinking back to his first day home. 'When I left the East End to go to stay with you all at Endeavour Downs in the Outback, I thought I'd never get used to it. I missed England even though I grew to love Australia despite the dust, the flies, the heat …'

That brought a memory back for Doris. 'The sweltering heat. The sweltering, sweltering heat.'

Michael suddenly became maudlin and nostalgic. 'That's right. The people we knew. But my, what a good bunch they all were.'

'In such a difficult climate,' Doris recalled, 'and in conditions they all battled so well. I have the greatest admiration for Roy, Josie and Terry of course. They chose such a hard way of life.'

'And they do it so well too,' Michael emphasised. 'Coming back here – everything is so much greener and softer.'

'I noticed that too.' This was the trigger to set Johnny off on another descriptive narration. 'I spent my arrival day just reacquainting myself with everything that was so British. The splendid silk green of the countryside, the lean cows and sheep in the fields, the fine oak timbers and skilfully woven thatched roofs of the village cottages, the smell of the fishing port and the algae green sea lapping over multi-coloured pearl shaded stones. When I took the train to London I sat wide eyed with excitement studying every nuance, every crevice, every dale and wood of the rural countryside as the steam from the locomotive soared backwards in an eternal silver-black line across a mild blue, cheerful sky.'

'The way you use words fascinates me Johnny,' Michael said. 'It's as if you're sensing every moment of life, absorbing every detail, sight and sound.'

Johnny gave him a smile, not perhaps of warmth but more of recognition for he had probably tapped the roof of his soul. He explained and in his soulful way his words were strung together in a pattern and patter Michael had never heard anyone repeat since.

'It's remarkable Michael but I truly believe that every day we learn something. Every day of our lives is to be savoured, tasted, enjoyed or experienced. From the bad times we taste sadness and defeat but we also learn to move on and try again. In the good times we reap the benefits that life has to offer. Not necessarily the riches. Even a simple train journey can be interesting. Take my journey up to London. It went through all manner of scenery, downs, hills, chalk pits, rectangular gold and green fields, and railway stations where proud stationmasters adorned the platforms with reams of colourful flowers in pots and baskets adding style to strata. I am given to wondering if there is a connection between the British steam railways and the wildlife and nature that seems to proliferate along the tracks. I noticed no end of animals. Doe-eyed rabbits bounced along by the edges of the rolling stock. A red vixen fox with its young grey curious cubs trailed through isolated cuttings that overflowed with gorse and flora. Yes, Michael, in the space of an ordinary day there are so many fine things worth noting. So much of life is special.'

The reunion went on all night until the next morning when Johnny left for Glasgow. They had talked about so much. They remembered so much. It was a wonderful reunion. So much of life is special. Such fine words, Johnny.

Twenty-One

Chichester, West Sussex 2006

The train pulled into Chichester station. Michael Forbes always felt pleased to return home to this rustic Roman town that typified so much of English history. Now, almost eighty years of age, he was grey-haired, bespectacled and smartly dressed in a black blazer and tie. He had softened with age. No longer a young gregarious Cockney, he had become in old age a mild mannered, slower man, happy in the memories of his long life and content with the family life that had brought him so much happiness.

In the sixty years since he had been an evacuee in Australia, Michael had never travelled abroad again except for a day trip to France from Jersey where he had been on holiday at the time. The holidays he had been on with his family and after being widowed were spent in the Lake District, Yorkshire, Scotland, Northumberland and the Channel Islands. It was when he walked through Chichester that Saturday afternoon he happened to cast his eyes on a travel agent's window. There was a poster showing gum trees and cattle on a red plain and in another corner there was a picture of Sydney Harbour Bridge and the pristine white sails of the Opera House. 'Come to Australia' the advertisement seemed to shout out.

On the walk through the town Michael's memory had been jogged and he thought of his life out there long ago. It hardly seemed possible did it that Michael should remember in terms of six decades ago. A lot of water had passed under the proverbial bridge since then. Oh my word it had. Good memories. Sad memories. Although that was what life was all about – was it not? Taking it all in one's stride, getting on with it and moving on to the chapter that follows.

He felt blessed. A long career in the medical services as an ambulance

165

driver had helped him provide for his wife and two children. Michael remembered the first time he had set eyes on his future wife. It was in the hop fields of Kent in that glorious season of 1939. He had been scrumping golden apples from a house and the young girl who lived there with her parents had surprised him. Her name was Margaret. Several years after the war Michael had spotted her at a dance in Maidstone. Three months later they got wed and together they had forty-five years of happy marriage; a union that produced two children. Michael's daughter worked as a doctor at St Richard's Hospital and from her marriage she had given Michael one grandson. Michael's son worked happily in a garden centre and his marriage had produced two grand-daughters who Michael doted on.

Chichester was bustling that afternoon. It was the height of the festival season and apart from the usual Saturday shoppers there were corner street buskers playing everything from classical to rock and Morris dancers performing as well as some Barbershop singers. It had been a long day since Michael had left Jersey and he was nearly home.

A quick shandy at his favourite pub The Mitre followed and then it was round the corner to his home in Worcester Road. It had been lonely since his wife had died but it was full of treasured memories, records, books and photographs. His record collection typified all the generations that had passed by since he was a boy. Almost every decade there was a singer that became synonymous with that era who indirectly influenced other entertainers of that generation. When their records were played it was possible to envisage the time, the personalities and where a person was when they first heard the music.

Among his collection of records there were LPs of the greats of their day: Al Jolson, Bing Crosby, Frank Sinatra, Perry Como, Tony Bennett, Nat King Cole, Elvis Presley and Matt Monro – all of them representing a time gone by. There were records too of singers whose careers had flashed and crackled momentarily: Johnny Ray, Hank Williams, Eddie Fisher, Frankie Laine, Guy Mitchell, 'Hutch' and Al Bowlly. If Michael listened to any of those the face of a relative or friend appeared in his memory.

Michael had recently been watching a series of Australian films on television that had revived the memories of his wartime years out there. He had seen *The Overlanders, Bush Christmas, Bitter Springs, Jeddah, On the Beach, They're a Weird Mob* and *Walkabout*. Late at night over a steaming hot cup of tea and a slice of toast and Marmite he had watched these old films usually starring Chips Rafferty or Bud Tingwell and as the scenes of peppercorn heat, stampeding cattle and hot big distances came across on the small screen Michael could almost taste and sense the atmosphere of a very special memory long ago.

He had learned much from the wonderful people he had known. They were all memories now. But not forgotten. They were still loved and cherished deep in his mind. From the long double windows of his lounge he had views of crisp green fields with golden patches. There were photographs in frames around the room. There was one of him on his wedding day to Maggie. There was one of Aunt Doris and Uncle Jack at Endeavour Downs Cattle Station. Also keeping him company were separate photographs of his beloved mother and father Honeysuckle and Frank. How he still missed them even after all these years.

Michael had been dreaming of days gone by as he dozed in his comfortable lounge room chair. He thought of his father Frank who always had such a battle with life. He used to work so hard for very little in return at the factory. Michael could see him now, happy as a lark in the hop fields in 1939. What a golden time! What a glorious season that was! He would never forget the night his father held centre stage at the hop pickers' last night party. Frank may only have been an ordinary working man but he died doing his best for his family. He died doing his bit for the country as an air raid warden. 'Dad, I was so proud of you,' thought Michael. He just wanted to say the words he had never really had the chance to.

They were lucky in that that they had wonderful support from Honeysuckle. She was kind, faithful, caring, gentle, strong, beautiful, loyal and generous. For some reason one of the strongest memories Michael had of his mother was of her singing to herself in the kitchen on that September Sunday morning in 1939 when they learned the nation was at war. 'I miss you, Mum. You were one splendid lady' Michael thought to himself and for a moment his tired old eyes clouded over with unwept tears at the warmth of her even after all these years.

Another couple who always aroused warm feelings within him whenever he thought of them were Spangler and Cherry Corrigan. Fun-loving, frivolous, faithful friends who never stopped laughing or enjoying themselves no matter how difficult life may have been. Good, kind, faithful friends who supported his Mum during the war. 'Bless you

Spangler and Cherry', he thought and he smiled. They could always make people smile. Even at the worst of times.

Aunt Doris and Jack Hope were made for each other. Doris was a wonderful Cockney rose, gentle and soft but with a spirit of iron. Uncle Jack with his warm Australian character was, in effect, the best man she could ever have married. He was also a gutsy man who had shown immense courage during the war. Some years after Doris had died Michael had gone through old letters and papers she had kept. Former prisoners-of-war had written of Jack's courage in keeping up morale among the men and standing up to his captors constantly. It was not clear how Jack had died but his commanding officer had written a statement open to interpretation. 'Jack Hope died as courageously as he had lived'. Doris never remarried after Jack. Not for the lack of suitors. Many a man would have laid his coat down Walter Raleigh-style for Doris. The truth was much simpler. She just never got over Jack.

Now the folk Michael knew in Australia, what a marvellous bunch they were! Roy, Josie and Terry Lane were three of the warmest people he ever knew. Roy was everything a good Australian was all about: decency, warmth, integrity, toughness without making a big show about it. Josie was his perfect counterpart. She had the same values. He thought that Terry would probably have the same strengths today.

Michael would never forget that cattle drive from Endeavour Downs, New South Wales to Ogilvie Junction, Queensland. Australia was so fond in his memory. Often he thought of those magnificent days on the trail beneath deep blue skies and horizon lines with only the ghostly shape of a gleaming gum tree standing in a state of solitude. He remembered spectacular red sunsets and the scent of eucalyptus and smoke rising from a campfire in the Outback somewhere beneath the Southern Cross in that rugged passionate land.

He remembered with much respect Don and Joe. They were two unique men of the bush. Don was the solitary rider, a man of industry and courage. Joe, who kept himself to himself, was the most fearless rider and jackaroo in the Outback. Wherever those two fine men were today he hoped that they would be as fearless and as strong as they were back then.

Freddie Bannan, now there was a name to conjure with. Freddie was described by Roy as 'one of the very best; a fun-loving, humours, hard-working larrikin who wouldn't want to be remembered any other way'. Michael could not top Roy's words. They were perfect.

Finally there was his old mate, Johnny McCullough. He was a rough diamond, travelling Scotsman with a lyrical way of speaking and a sensitive heart. 'What a fellow, eh!'

Michael felt privileged to have known these fine people who were so much part of his memory; these battling spirits and kindly hearts, born of the fruit of the spirit. How much he learnt from them all about the things in life that count the most; love of your fellow human being, friendship, trust, loyalty, courage under pressure, the ability to fight on in life and to rise above humiliation, disappointment and struggle. For truly amid the measure of the years, life yields wonderful moments which are treasured forever in memory.

He thought of himself as a young boy riding with Terry Lane on the cattle drive. It was the time of his life. The experience he would always remember to the end of his days. He remembered a poem by Banjo Patterson that Freddie Bannan had once read to him over a campfire. Even after all these years he could hear the voice of Freddie reading lines from 'The Man from Snowy River'.

> 'There was movement at the station, for the word had passed around,
> That the colt from old Regret had got away,
> And had joined the wild bush horses – he was worth a thousand pound,
> So all the cracks had gathered to the fray.
> All the tried and noted riders from the stations near and far
> Had mustered at the homestead overnight,
> For the bushmen love hard riding where the wild bush horses are
> And the stock-horse snuffs the battle with delight.
> There was Harrison, who made his pile when Pardon won the Cup,
> The old man with his hair as white as snow.
> But few could ride beside him when his blood was fairly up –
> He would go wherever horse and man could go.
> And Clancy of the Overflow came down to lend a hand,
> No better horseman ever held the reins,
> For never horse could throw him while the saddle-girths would stand,
> He learnt to ride while droving the plains'

Michael opened his eyes and smiled. 'Droving on the plains. Did he really do those things? How wonderful'.

Also by the Author

Love Across the Decades

Colour Sergeant Chesney V.C.

Come Sing with Me My People

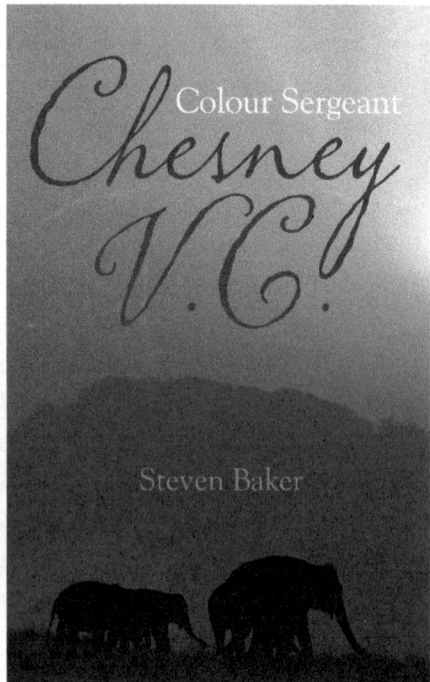